TIME'S RELATIVE

DEBBIE DE LOUISE

D1569117

In memory of my two beloved cats, Floppy and Holly, who were featured in this book and for everyone who wishes they could travel through time to change something in their life.

AUTHOR'S NOTE

I wrote this book twenty years ago and came across it with many other manuscripts, some of which were still handwritten in notebooks. Luckily, this was on computer but needed to be updated and reformatted in the current version of Word. At first, I also considered updating the period information but decided to keep it and the 1998 setting. I thought this would be appropriate because it was a time-travel piece. Readers may find of interest the additional information I added later in the book of major events that occurred after the book was written until the present day including a brief scene describing the COVID-19 pandemic.

PROLOGUE

Through the canyon wall, she saw a refraction of light. A shiny object was wedged between two orange rocks. She hoped it was the disk. She scrambled up the hill, nearly losing her footing as she hurried forward. She felt time pressing against her, its heavy weight holding her back as she took each higher step. At the top of the hill, she paused, looking down from the dizzying height at the pebbles that had slid to the bottom. She felt like one of those pebbles – that at any moment she might fall to her fate, an insignificant digression in time's path.

She forced these thoughts from her mind as she reached for the glowing object, sheltered between the two highest rocks. Her fingers brushed the tiny buttons while she carefully removed the disk from its lodging. She held her breath when the time-travel apparatus slipped into her cupped hands. She knew she had to destroy it.

She could toss it down the hill hoping it would break upon impact with the ground below or knock it against the rocks surrounding her until its microchips shattered into harmless pieces. She only knew she had to act soon before her stalker caught up with her.

The disk felt suddenly pounds heavier as she raised it toward the rock from where she'd extracted it. The first blow made a tiny dent on the left side, the second cracked off part of the turning wheel. Buoyed by newfound momentum, Sam pounded the disk against the rock until pieces of it flew off, one cutting into the side of her palm. Bleeding from the wound, Sam didn't stop.

The final blow Sam administered to the tiny machine caused her to stumble backward. She dropped the broken disk as she fell, grabbing one of the rocks she'd used as a foothold on her way up the hill. Her right hand was bleeding badly now as the rock she grasped tore open the scratch from the disk. As she groped her way to a standing position, she felt a tremor ride up the hill. Had her fall dislodged enough rock to cause an avalanche? It would be ironic if she dies trying to save her future.

CHAPTER ONE
NEW YORK CITY, SEPTEMBER 14, 1998

"The beginning is the most important part of the work."

— PLATO: "THE REPUBLIC"

The job ad placed by a company called Virtual Software in Garden City sounded ideal. *"Wanted: Computer literate individual with research skills and a background in history. Willing and able to travel extensively all expenses paid. Potential to earn six-figure income. Apply in person 9-3 September 14-15."*

The ad appeared in yesterday's Sunday paper that she'd just picked up to read this morning. Today was September 14, and already someone might have been hired for the job.

Samantha Stewart circled the address in the ad in red. A month ago, she would never have contemplated looking through the New York Times for a new position. But that was before the breakup. Because of Peter, she couldn't return to the small business library she'd called home for the last five years. He was the senior accountant of a firm that frequently used the reference books and databases of the Morgan Business Library.

Samantha frowned as she tapped the capped end of the red marker on her kitchen table. The sound as it struck the oak

3

echoed staccato in the silence not unlike that of a breaking drumstick. The truth was that the end of her relationship with Peter Clark was the proverbial straw that broke the camel's back. She needed a change in her professional life. As much as she enjoyed her work, the Morgan Business Library was a dead end. Once you knew to which books to direct the patrons, the challenge was gone. The questions changed, but the answers were often the same. Then there was the technology situation. Sam had never been afraid of computers and had even welcomed the coming of the "Information Age." All the more reason why she couldn't stay at MBL. The constant fighting for funds and competition for grants left her frustrated and angry. Hell, the library was still using a 486. They had only one Internet connection. There was no room to grow but out.

Sam read the ad again. She certainly had the requirements. She was computer literate to the degree she didn't need to use any of the "dummy" or "idiot" books. Her research skills had always been excellent, the main reason she'd chosen to major in library science after graduating with a history degree from the State University. Another plus, according to the ad. Then there was her willingness and ability to travel on someone else's money. That was a definite incentive. Although Sam would hardly be considered a world traveler, she loved visiting new places and meeting new people. Like the plot of a good novel, there was something special about escaping the routine and changing one's view. She'd been stuck in one place for too long. She yearned for the opportunity to get away that this job offered. And a six-income figure? What library position ever paid that? On the other hand, her cynical side warned her that the ad might be some sort of scam. Virtual Software? She'd never heard of it.

Samantha decided to Google the company on her computer. If her search didn't turn up anything, then she'd resort to going to the Morgan library. She hadn't been there since she quit in early August, and she wasn't looking forward to running into Peter, or, worse, her replacement. She should've been smarter and done what all the career books advised and found a job before she quit her old one. Still, it was only herself she had to worry about. She amended that — herself and her cat, Holly. She looked down at the orange and white tabby she'd rescued from the North Shore Animal League two years ago right before Christmas, thus the name "Holly" for holidays. Some people said owners began to look like their pets after a certain amount of time spent together. She and Holly already looked alike with their red hair and green eyes. Both were petite with slender arms and legs.

"Oh, Holly," Samantha said, picking up the cat who purred at her touch. "I can afford your cat food a little while longer on the money I've saved, but I think I have to start serious job hunting."

The cat put out her orange paw and knocked the marker out of Sam's hand. "I know you want to play, but Mommy has to think of our future."

Sam went over to the computer she'd set up in the living room/den of her small apartment. Holly followed behind, jumping on the desk, and trotting over the keyboard. Above the desk hung framed photos of the cat done by Sam's best friend, a professional photographer.

"Stop. I have work to do, Holly!"

The cat looked up with pleading green eyes and mouthed a meow that would break a cat lover's heart.

"When I finish, we'll play. I promise."

The cat jumped down and stalked off. Minutes later, Sam heard the tossing of a fur mouse as Holly played by herself.

"Good girl. Keep yourself amused like you did when I worked full-time. You've become spoiled these last few weeks having me around as your playmate."

Sam had considered getting Holly a companion cat, but her apartment was barely big enough for one cat, and she didn't know if the very possessive Holly would take well to a new cat in her territory.

She logged onto the Internet and waited as the modem

screeched out its connection. When Netscape opened, she searched Yahoo for any websites that matched "Virtual Software." Her search yielded too many results, so she narrowed it to "Virtual Software" "Garden City." To her surprise, one of the site matches seemed to hit the target. She clicked on the link for "Virtual Software Company, Garden City, New York" and was taken to the home page of the company.

Virtual Software had opened its doors two years ago. Specializing in mapping and travel-related software, the company showed a gross income of $16 million. *Not bad*, Samantha thought, clicking on the link labeled "staff." Only two names were listed: Gregory Parsons and Jane Oldsfield. A brief biography and photo followed each.

Jane was the president and founder of the company. Her photo showed an attractive, dark-haired woman in her early to mid-thirties. Her biography read like a valedictorian's resume: graduated Yale in '85 with dual bachelor's degrees in physics and computer science; spent five years teaching both those subjects at MIT; spent another five years working as a research assistant and earning a Master's degree in telecommunications technology from MIT; relocated to the North Shore of Long Island in '96 to start Virtual Software.

Samantha continued reading. Gregory Parsons' bio was briefer but only a bit less noteworthy. The vice-president of Virtual Software had graduated from Stamford the same year Samantha received her degrees from Yale, but his undergraduate work had been in communications. He'd received a journalism degree before taking a job as an editor for a scientific journal called *Science Professional*. After five years, he, too, went back to school for a master's degree in telecommunications from MIT. *"And that's where their paths must have crossed,"* Samantha mused as she studied the photo of the bearded, sandy blond-haired man with dark blue eyes as fathomless as the ocean on a stormy night.

The rest of Virtual Software Company's home page didn't tell her much. The company had produced several award-winning programs but seemed to prefer to keep its name out of the news industry's spotlight. Although its main office was based on Long Island, there were other offices scattered throughout the East Coast. The information was scant, and Samantha decided to try to dig up more data before making an application with the company. As much as she dreaded it, she knew it would be worth a shot to check some of the sources at the Morgan Library. Disconnecting her Internet connection and shutting down her computer, Samantha prepared to take the short walk to the MLB. Holly slept on the couch, curled into an orange ball, having given up on playtime. Sam tiptoed quietly by her, but the cat's sharp ears flattened even while her eyes remained shut.

It wasn't quite noon yet on this second Monday of September, and, although the streets were already packed with noisy and foul-emitting city traffic, Samantha enjoyed the eight-block walk to the library. The touch of coolness on the air after the sweltering New York summer gave her steps a lift. Fall in the city was a wonderful time. But what if she were hired at this software company and sent off to do some of the advertised extensive travel? What city or town might she end up in to celebrate autumn? Samantha laughed at herself for her imagination. Even if the position hadn't been filled yet, there would surely be plenty of competition for the promise of a six-figure income. Besides, after investigating the company further, she might find that the advertisement was a scam after all, or that the position just wasn't for her.

Samantha was so deep in thought she was almost run down by a taxi that made a sharp turn after the walk sign hand came on. When she'd passed safely to the other side of the street and was within doors of the brick building that housed the Morgan Business Library, she continued her musings. It wasn't as if she were about to accept the first job she was offered. In the past month, she'd been on several interviews. She'd been on the verge of accepting the NYPL's offer, but something had made her decline. That same something seemed to spark her interest in the software company position.

Samantha stepped through the doorway of the library and into the ambience of a small private club. Dark wood-paneled walls lined with books surrounded her as one of her ex-co-workers, Derek Brand, approached. "Sam, my dear. How are you?"

"Okay for an unemployed single woman with a cat to support. How are you, Derek?"

The tall, lanky man with horn-rimmed glasses smiled, showing front teeth that should have had the attention of an orthodontist thirty years earlier. "I'm managing to survive without you, but it isn't easy. Every time I go into the stacks, I picture you there."

"Sorry to be such a heartbreaker," she teased. Derek had been a good friend while she'd worked at MBL, but they both knew she'd had no romantic interest in him. He was a sweet, book-loving man in his early forties who still lived with his elderly widowed mother and a cocker spaniel named Shakespeare.

"Have they hired my replacement yet?" she asked.

"No one could replace you." He mimicked a sniffle. "No. The budget's so tight I think they'll just add your workload to mine unless you're ready to come back."

"I don't think so. In fact, I may have an interview tomorrow. That's why I'm here. I need to do some research on a Long Island company called Virtual Software."

"You know where to look," Derek said, apparently reluctant to lend a hand in helping her gather information about a job that would make her termination at the Morgan Library permanent.

Before Samantha could reply, a man in a tailored gray business suit came up to the Reference Desk to ask Derek a question. Samantha slipped away toward the business resources.

Scouring the main directories, Samantha didn't learn much more about Virtual Software than what she'd dug up on the

Internet. However, when she did a name search for "Oldsfield, Jane" in the business and newspaper periodicals computer database, a recent article entitled "Software Company President Missing" appeared on the screen. Samantha hit the Enter Key to read the full text of the article which had been featured in the July 21 issue of the *Long Island Newsday*. A strange feeling overcame her as she read about the disappearance of "Ms. Jane Oldsfield, Yale graduate and president of Virtual Software, a Garden City-based producer of travel software." The article was brief but more than enough to stir her librarian's research instincts.

"Ms. Jane Oldsfield, a 33-year-old Yale and MIT graduate who is president/founder of Virtual Software, a Garden City-based producer of travel software, has been reported missing by Gregory Parsons, vice-president of the company. Parsons said that Oldsfield didn't report to work on Monday morning, July 20, nor did she answer any phone calls to her house in Old Brookville. Upon further investigation by the Nassau County Police, it was determined that Oldsfield had vacated her home hurriedly, without taking any of her belongings, sometime during the weekend of July 18-19. Oldsfield, originally from the Boston area, doesn't have any family that could be contacted. Parsons, who last saw her at work on Friday, July 17, commented that she'd seemed preoccupied by something, but he wouldn't elaborate. "As long as I've known Jane since our days at MIT, she's been a very private person," he said. A continued search for Oldsfield's whereabouts is planned by the Nassau County Police."

Samantha was shocked. Something in Denmark was fishy. And, if she were smart, she'd get out of the water before one of those fish bit her. But, having gone this far, like the proverbial cat, she needed to satisfy her curiosity. She checked to see if there'd been any further follow-up articles on Jane Oldsfield's disappearance. She wanted to know if the president of the company she was considering interviewing with had ever been found, and if so, had she been found alive?

"You sure look absorbed. Find anything interesting?" Derek was through helping the businessman and stood next to her computer. His nearness unnerved her.

"A few things, but you know me, I don't quit until I find everything I'm looking for."

"What are you looking for?" Derek's myopic eyes squinted at the computer screen. She hoped he wasn't actually reading the text. She could've sighed with relief when he glanced away at his multiple time-zone wristwatch before exclaiming, "Well, I'm going to lunch soon. I'll leave you to your hunt unless you'd care to join me."

"No thanks. Maybe next time."

"Right. Well, good luck on your interview."

He strode away toward his desk. Samantha continued reading. There was another article about Jane Oldsfield written a week later than the first, but this one didn't solve the mystery. The headline read, "Virtual Software President is 'Virtually' Missing."

Samantha was so intrigued by the story that she nearly disturbed the older gentleman at a table next to her when she began reading it aloud to herself.

"Ms. Jane Oldsfield, president of Virtual Software of Garden City, who disappeared early last week from her Old Brookville home, is still missing. The Nassau County Police have no leads. Oldsfield was reported missing on July 20 by her co-worker and vice-president of the travel software company, Greg Parsons."

That was it. Samantha spent another half-hour trying to locate additional articles without any luck.

Before Derek returned and before her hunger cravings worsened or Peter dropped by for an unwelcome visit, Samantha decided to break for lunch to reevaluate what she'd learned so far. She left the library and walked home where she found a hungry animal waiting at the front door.

"Calm down, Holly," she told the cat that was meowing pitifully for food. "You just ate a few hours ago. My gosh! If you keep this up, you'll lose your figure."

She opened a can of Friskies cat food and emptied that along with some dry Meow Mix into two cat bowls in her kitchen. Then she made herself a tuna sandwich on pita bread and took a seat at the table. It was hard to believe she'd first learned about Virtual Software only that morning in the paper and had already unraveled a mystery about one of the company's officers. If the president of the company was still missing, then the vice-president was probably running the company and doing the interviewing for the advertised position. She thought of the photo of Greg Parsons that she'd seen on the Internet. The photo added nothing to the biography. Who was Greg Parsons? And who was Jane Oldsfield? More importantly, where was Jane Oldsfield?

CHAPTER TWO

"The past is a ghost, the future a dream. All we have is now."

— BILL COSBY

H olly, having abandoned her cat food after a few nibbles, jumped on the kitchen table, eyeing the human morsels.

"Holly, what did I tell you about sitting on the table? I know you love tuna, but this is my food."

The green eyes were mournful.

"Oh, here, you can have a little bit. I'm such a softy." Samantha speared a piece of tuna with her fork and put it on a paper plate that she placed on the floor. The cat immediately jumped down and gobbled up the goodies.

Cats have such one-track minds, Samantha thought, *Food, sleep, and play. If only life were that simple for people.*

Before she could contemplate the advantages of being born feline as opposed to homosapien, Samantha's phone rang. Getting up and answering it from the wall next to the refrigerator, she heard her friend Angie's voice.

"Hey, Sam, can you come out and play? I was thinking of

doing some shooting this afternoon at Washington Square Park. Then maybe we can grab a bite for dinner in the Village."

Angela Palmer had been Sam's friend since she'd first moved to the city nine years ago. Samantha had been working at the Queensborough Public Library then. They met when Angela came in for some photography books. A freelance photographer for several New York travel and entertainment magazines, Angie had left an unhappy home in Chicago for a better life in the "Big Apple." She seemed to have found it or made it depending on how you looked at it. At twenty-nine, the blonde-haired photographer earned twice Samantha's salary and was engaged to a doctor.

"Sure," Sam said. "I just came back from MBL. I was doing some research on a company I might interview with."

"Really." Angie sounded curious. "Tell me all about it over dinner. Can you be at the park in an hour?"

"No problem. See you then, Angie."

"Righto. Oh, by the way, Sam, you didn't run into Peter, did you?"

"No, but I wasn't disappointed."

"Good girl. You're finally getting over that bastard."

"You always thought he was one, and you were right. How's Mark?"

"Working twenty-five hours a day as usual, but I'm so busy getting ready for the wedding I don't really mind. He'll be taking off two weeks in November for our honeymoon. I can't wait to get to the Islands. I've got to run, sweetie. See you at four. Bye."

"Bye."

At four o'clock, Sam sat on a bench looking at the still green leaves of the trees shading Washington Square Park. Angie was always notoriously late for all appointments. Sam, on the other hand, was always early. She'd been sitting on the bench since a quarter to four.

Surprises of all surprises, Angie appeared on time for once carrying her Nikon on her shoulder in her black camera bag. "Hey, Sam!"

"You're early for you."

Angie laughed, showing perfect white teeth. She pushed a strand of her long blonde hair away from her cheek and tilted her head to reposition her floppy bangs. "I'm really eager to hear about this new job. I also want to get some good snaps before it gets dark. I hate this time of year when daylight fades so early."

"We have plenty of time till darkness. The clocks haven't been turned back yet. They don't do that until the end of October now. And, Angie, there is no new job yet. I saw an ad, and I might go on the interview."

Angie zipped opened her camera case and handed the empty case to Sam as she set up her camera paraphernalia. "Sounds pretty serious to me when you're already researching the company and even returned to MBL at the risk of running into Peter Perfect."

Samantha laughed. Peter Perfect was the nickname Angie had given Peter because he was such a perfectionist and expected others to be also. "I always research everything, Angie, like you always photograph everything."

Angie took some pictures of the trees and a couple kissing on a bench on the farther side of the park. She turned at that remark and snapped Samantha.

"Don't do that!" Sam exclaimed. "You know I'm not photogenic."

"You don't have to be photogenic. You're natural, Sam. I respect that. Mark's that way, too. That's why I'm marrying him. You don't find too many natural people these days."

Samantha changed the subject, fearing Angie would bring up Peter again or Roger, her ex-husband who'd put her in a hospital in Chicago before she'd left him less than a year after the marriage.

"So, where do you want to go to dinner, Miss Palmer?"

Angie snapped pictures of the pigeons tap dancing along the promenade. "I was thinking of one of the Internet cafes in the Village. They're getting more popular now, and I'd love to see what it's like to surf the net while I chow down."

"Angie! I didn't think you were into computers."

"I have to be. Everyone has to be these days. I've even been thinking of taking some continuing ed classes in digital photography."

"Sounds like a good idea. By the way, this company I'm thinking of interviewing with is a software company."

Angie came over and joined Sam on the bench, lowering her camera to her lap. "Really? I thought you were a librarian."

"I am. The position I'd be interviewing for involves research. The benefits sound great — paid travel, six-figure income..."

"Wow! Where is this job? I'll interview with you if you don't mind the competition."

"There'll be plenty of competition. I'm sure of that. Even if I'm chosen, I don't know if I'd take it. It might be a scam. It sounds too good. And, Angie, get this, the president of the company, a female Yale graduate, has been missing since July."

Angie's large blue eyes widened. "Oh, my gosh, Sam. I have to hear the rest. We'll talk about me over dinner, boring wedding plans and stuff."

Sam hesitated. Maybe she'd told her friend too much already. It was always bad luck to talk about a job before the interview. Nonsense. She wasn't sure she wanted it; and a second opinion from someone as worldly astute as Angie, might be worth it. "Well," she began, "there's not so much to tell yet. I saw the ad in Sunday's paper which I read this morning."

"And you accuse me of procrastinating," Angie said.

"I don't accuse you of procrastinating. I accuse you of always being late. Today was a fluke."

"How do you know? I may have turned over a new leaf. Talk about leaves ..." Angie aimed her camera at the tree nearest their bench. "Wait until next month. I can't wait to shoot the autumn leaves."

"I thought you wanted to hear my story."

"I sure do, and I'm listening. I'm also working, but I can do two things at once. I'm a great multi-tasker."

Sam held back a laugh. "Well, this company, Virtual Software, produces travel software programs. They're looking for someone with research skills and a history background to work in their research department. The job is supposed to involve a lot of travel."

Angie took a cloth out of the pocket of her designer jeans and wiped the front of her camera lens. "Why history? What does that have to do with travel?"

"Lots. People who travel usually like to know the background of an area, and there are many historic sites all over the country — and the world for that matter."

"I don't know. Sounds strange. What did you find out at the MBL?"

"What I've already told you. Their president, a woman named Jane Oldsfield, disappeared from her Brookville home in July. According to the latest information I found, she hasn't turned up yet."

"Wow!" Angie clicked a few shots of the Oak and put her camera in its case. "Brookville? Isn't that on Long Island?"

"That's right. I might stop and pay my mom a visit while I'm out there."

Angie laughed. "Oh, she'll be thrilled. When was the last time you talked with your mother?"

"Yesterday. I usually call her a few times a week."

"Good girl. I wish I had a mother to call or visit."

"Please, Angie, don't reprimand me. My mother makes me feel guilty enough. But it's not like she's alone or anything. My sister, the moocher, still lives there and probably will forever."

"I'd say I wish I had a sister, too, but you know about my family."

Sam had to change the subject. She knew too well the sad story of how Angie's family had perished in a fire in a suburb of Chicago when she was five. As an only survivor of that tragedy, she was raised in an orphanage before she "escaped" at fifteen to live with the man she later married and who nearly killed her in one of his drunken rages.

"I'm sorry, Angie. I promise I'll try to be a better daughter and sister. But, if you don't mind, I'd like to discuss dinner now. Which Internet café did you have in mind?"

"I don't recall its name, but I have the address in my camera bag. It's pretty close." She glanced at her watch. "It's not even five. Are you sure you want to eat so early?"

"I had a light lunch with Holly hanging over my shoulder, so I'm a bit hungry."

"How is that cute fur person of yours? Is she ready for another photo session yet?"

Angie had photographed Holly from kittenhood and given Sam the framed photos to hang in her apartment. A true ham, Holly enjoyed her photo sessions with Angie but wouldn't sit still for any of the pictures Sam tried to take of her.

"I have enough photos of Miss Holly right now. Thank you."

Sam and Angie walked to the restaurant, dodging rush hour traffic as they crossed Washington Square. Internet Bytes was a small brownstone building hidden in a niche on a street occupied by motorcyclists sporting reptilian tattoos. A hippie-looking woman with stringy dark hair seated them at a table while Janis Joplin played from hidden speakers.

The square black and white parquet tables had paper menus that served as placemats. The computers were in the back of the restaurant. Five IBM compatible Pentiums were occupied by an assorted group of diners, many of whom seemed to belong to the bikers' congregation on the block.

"There's one computer available," Angie pointed out as she took a seat at the table.

The hippie waitress smiled, contorting her unpainted lips in what didn't exactly pass as a happy expression. "Surfing is by appointment only. If you want one after dinner, I'll have to take your names."

Angie didn't wait to ask Sam. "Reserve it under Palmer and Stewart, like Cagney and Lacey, only prettier."

The waitress didn't comment. Instead, she scribbled their names on the notepad she carried and asked, "Before I take your dinner orders, what would you like to drink? I recommend the flavored mineral water."

Angie picked up the placemat. "I'll try the strawberry one. What about you, Sam?"

Sam skimmed the list of dyed soda water. "Do you have Sprite?"

The waitress grimaced. It gave her a menacing appearance. "No. But we carry Classic Coke."

You're a Classic, Sam thought. "That'll be fine," she replied putting down her menu. She couldn't wait to see what type of solid food they offered.

After the waitress walked away to get their drinks from the bar across the room that had an equally eclectic group of patrons seated at stools in front of it, Sam glanced at the menu's main entree listings.

"So, what are you in the mood for, Angie, a Home Page Hero or a tasty Chicken.com platter?"

"I don't know. I might splurge and have the Browser Burger or the Manicotti Marinara a la Modem."

Sam decided on the chicken platter, while Angie chose the high-tech pasta dish. When their food arrived, shortly after their drinks, Sam said, "So, what about the wedding stuff? You promised you'd tell all at dinner."

Angie's fork was poised over what looked like a regular serving of Manicotti, Stouffer's style, minus the modem. At Sam's question, her face flushed slightly under the light tan which would be gone the following month. "Everything's under control — the florist, limo, chapel, even the photographer. Since I can't shoot my own wedding, I've chosen someone I've worked with who is top notch. I'm so excited, Sam. I never had a real wedding with Roger. I'm even wearing white, and I don't care. By the way, have you gone for all your fittings yet?"

Sam nodded. "I sure have. Now I just need to make sure I don't gain any weight between now and November 7." She looked down at her plate of chicken breasts in a cream sauce that tasted like a blend of Swiss cheese and sour cream. "This is actually pretty good. How's yours?"

"I've tasted better, but this isn't an Italian restaurant. I might've been wiser sticking to a tried-and-true American favorite like you did." Angie, a picky eater, never ate more than a few bites of any food. It showed on her figure that was perfect for her five-foot-five frame. If she'd been a few inches taller, Sam thought she would've made a great model, a Christie Brinkley type.

Sam picked up the conversation where it had sidetracked. "I really love the sky-blue bridesmaid's outfits you chose."

"I knew you would. The color will look terrific on you. I just hope you have a date by then."

Sam laughed. "I'm working on it, but first I have to find a job so I can afford your wedding gift."

"Talking about jobs," Angie pushed away her almost full plate. "Are you almost done, so we can surf the net? I'd love to see the home page of that company you were telling me about."

Sam moved her plate aside also. She'd managed to eat a good enough portion of the chicken so that the waitress wouldn't ask her if she wanted it wrapped to bring home. She didn't ask either one of them, even though Angie's plate was the perfect

19

candidate for a doggie bag. Instead, the woman asked, "Would you like to see our dessert menu?"

Angie raised a pale eyebrow to Sam who shook her head. "No, thanks. We can't eat anything else." Angie never ate dessert.

When the bill arrived, they negotiated who would pick up the tab and tip. Angie used her American Express to pay the bill because she'd issued the invitation, while Sam left a tip generous enough to offset the cost of the waitress' bangle bracelet collection.

Angie was the first to get up and motion toward the computers. "Let's go, Sam."

They sat on a cheap pair of uncomfortable desk chairs that had probably been bought at an office outlet clearance sale for damaged furniture. The ugly green plastic seats wobbled on their metal supports.

"If I fall and break something before my wedding, I'll sue this place," Angie exclaimed trying to center herself in the chair to keep her equilibrium.

The guy with the buzz cut and tattoo of a snake on his hefty left arm, looked away from the screen where he'd typed in the search term "Chain Gang" in the Yahoo dialog box. "Hey, Sis, don't sweat it. I'll give you my seat," he said getting up to tower above Angie.

"Thank you, but that isn't necessary. I think I've mastered this."

The biker twitched one of the earrings he wore and returned to his search.

Angie opened Netscape Navigator and asked Sam for Virtual Software's web address. After Angie typed the Virtual software's URL in the "open" box of the browser, the travel software company's home page appeared on the screen.

"This is great," Angie said. "I have to find a way to make my own home page for my photography. I could put up samples of my work."

"You could also put up a photo of yourself that will sell to a lot of the male population."

"Oh, stop that! You're no ugly duckling yourself, Miss Stewart."

"No, but I'm not model material. I'd rather put Holly's photo on my page."

Angie clicked on the arrows at the right side of the screen to scroll down the home page. When she saw the link for the company officers, she clicked on it and gave such a loud sigh when Greg Parsons' picture appeared that the man who'd offered her his seat looked at the two women with an expression Sam didn't want to decipher.

"He's gorgeous," Angie said. "Oooh, Sam, you have to go on that interview just to meet him."

"He is sort of sexy in an intellectual sort of way, but I bet he's married."

"I don't think so. There's no mention of a wife in his bio."

"I noticed that, too. Look, Angie, I've already seen all this. Are there any other sites you'd like to visit?"

"Well, I could visit some of the travel sites for the Bahamas but that might spoil the honeymoon."

"I doubt it. But if you don't mind, I'm getting a headache. I'd like to go home."

"Party pooper! Well, I guess it's okay. I have a Tylenol if you need one."

"Thanks, but I think I'm just tired."

Angie logged off and shut down the computer. Then she got up and tossed her camera bag over her shoulder. "I should get these developed tonight, anyway."

As Sam joined her and they started leaving the restaurant, the tattooed man winked at them. Angie waved goodbye to him.

"You shouldn't have encouraged that guy," Sam told her when they were out on the street.

"Who? Oh, the chain-gang member. I wasn't encouraging him; I was just being friendly. He was nice enough to offer me his chair."

"What am I going to do with you, Angie?"

"Take me to your interview tomorrow. I'll pretend I'm interested in the position, but I'll make sure I don't get it."

"Are you kidding?" They were walking across Washington Square which was already enshrouded in the semi-darkness that heralds twilight.

"I'm totally serious. C'mon, I'm free all morning tomorrow. What's the worst thing that can happen?"

"You see me make a fool of myself when I go there, and the position is already filled."

"Then we go out to breakfast, and I'll find us a nice spot where I can take photos of men, and you can pick up one."

"You are kidding."

"A little, but I'm serious about the breakfast."

They'd turned onto Sam's apartment block. "What if I get the job?"

"Then you buy breakfast."

Sam asked Angie if she wanted to come in for a while to visit with her favorite cat "niece" before heading back to the studio apartment she shared with Mark in Soho.

"Of course. Aunt Angie has been a pretty neglectful aunt. Since I've been busy with all the wedding preparations, I haven't had much time for my kitty niece, Holly."

Sam fumbled with her key in the lock. When she finally opened the door, an orange face with huge green eyes peered up at her and Angie as they entered the apartment.

"Hello, Princess," Angie said stooping to pet Holly's head. Holly rubbed her cheek against Angie's hand. "I've missed you, sweetie."

Sam put her purse down on her couch and went over to the

answering machine set up next to the computer on her desk by the window. "I had a telephone message while I was out," she said. "I'd better listen to it. It might be Mom."

"Probably is," Angie said, scratching behind Holly's ear. The cat purred loudly, eating up all the attention. "Call her back and tell her we'll visit her tomorrow. I always enjoy seeing Mrs. Stewart."

Sam pressed rewind and then the play button to listen to the message. She expected to hear her mother's anxious voice. Instead, another woman's voice played from the tape.

"This is a message for Samantha Stewart. Stay away from Virtual Software. If you go on that interview tomorrow, you'll be sorry."

The machine clicked off, leaving Sam bewildered. "What in the world was that all about?"

Angie abandoned Holly for the moment and came over to the desk. "I hate to sound like someone in Casablanca, but play it again, Sam."

Sam replayed the message, while the two women sat in silence except for Holly who cried for attention as she stood between them.

"Who could that be?" Angie asked. "Who else have you told about this job, Sam?"

"No one. That's the weird thing. You're the only one I've said a word to, Angie." Her voice choked. "Do you think I should call the police?"

"No, but I'm glad I'm going with you tomorrow."

"Wait a second. That was a warning. If someone wants me to stay away from that company, I'm going to oblige."

"And make whoever's playing a crank on you happy? No, Sam, I think you should go, and I'm going with you."

Holly had given up on the two humans and gone to play with one of her fur mice in the kitchen.

"In fact," Angie continued, "I'm going to stay with you here tonight, so we can get an early start."

Sam sighed. "That isn't necessary, Angie. I'll be okay. Besides, won't Mark miss your warm body next to his?"

"He gets in so late these days that I'm already asleep when he comes home. I'll call him, of course, but he'll understand."

"Okay, if you insist."

"I do, and I also insist that you stay in your bed while I sleep on the couch."

Sam, knowing there was no arguing with Angie who could be quite stubborn at times, relented. Although she didn't want to admit it, she felt better about having her friend stay over after the crank call.

CHAPTER THREE

"Time flies over us but leaves its shadow behind."

— NATHANIEL HAWTHORNE

Sam and Angie were like two teenagers at a slumber party. They watched late-night TV with a bowl of microwave popcorn between them, talked about guys, and took turns playing "Mouse" with Holly. Neither of them brought up the following day's interview or the anonymous caller.

Around midnight, Sam yawned and heaved herself off the couch. "I'm beat, Angie. I think it's off to bed for me." She'd already given Angie an extra set of sheets for the couch and had changed into the oversized cat T-shirt she used as a nightshirt. On the front of the white shirt was a tabby kitten sleeping on a pillow who looked like a younger Holly. In a cloud above the cat, were several mice the cat was dreaming of. "I might have another nightshirt you can use," she offered as she made her way into her bedroom.

"Don't bother," Angie called back finishing off the last fully popped kernel of corn and bringing the bowl of seeds and burnt kernels into the kitchen where she dumped them in the trash bin and rinsed the bowl out in the sink. "I can sleep in these clothes. They're actually quite comfortable."

"Well, okay. Goodnight, Angie."

"Goodnight, Sam."

Sam didn't know what time it was when she heard the laughter. She was still drowsy, awakening from some fragments of forgotten dreams. She vaguely recalled Angie volunteering to stay over that night and the time they'd spent together before bedtime. Since the laughter was a woman's and seemed to be coming from the living room, Sam assumed it was Angie laughing at one of Holly's antics, since the cat wasn't in her usual spot curled up next to Sam on the bed. The problem was that the laughter didn't sound like Angie's. It was loud and throaty, almost eerie in its pitch.

Sam sat up in bed and pulled her sheets aside. "Angie, is that you? What's going on?"

There was no reply.

Sam got up and slipped on furry white cat slippers that had once really spooked Holly. Now she was the one who was spooked. Slipping quietly from the room, she tiptoed toward the living room. The couch was unoccupied and looked as if it had never been slept in. Even the sheets she'd left for Angie were nowhere around. The laughter seemed to have stopped as soon as she'd left the bedroom, but the sound still echoed in her ears like the screech of chalk along a blackboard.

Sam was about to call out to her friend again, when a breeze from the window she didn't realize she'd left open caused her to turn and see a figure in black holding her cat.

Sam was too scared to scream. In her hurry to find out what was happening in the living room, she hadn't stopped to turn on a light. The dark figure laughed that chilling laugh she'd heard before, and Holly cried out with a plaintive meow that stirred her owner.

"Who are you? What do you want?" Sam asked in a voice groggy from both sleep and fear.

"I told you," the woman said. "If you go tomorrow, you'll be sorry." From the shadows, Sam couldn't see the woman's face – but the voice was the same as the telephone caller.

"Where's Angie?"

Sam wasn't sure she'd heard the woman's reply correctly. "She's where I was a few minutes ago. I switched with her; but don't worry, she'll be back. She won't even know she's been anywhere else." Holly squirmed in the woman's arms, finally convincing her to let her down. "Take your cat. I don't need another one. Now remember about tomorrow." With that, the woman turned and took from her skirt pocket a round object the size of a golf ball. Sam feared it was a gun, but it apparently wasn't a weapon. As soon as the woman touched it, she disappeared, and Angie lay asleep on the couch under the sheets Sam had given her.

Holly jumped up on Angie's stomach and kneaded the covers. Angie awoke to see Sam standing over her. "What's wrong, Sam? Did you have a bad dream?"

Sam didn't know how she could explain to her friend what had just happened when she couldn't understand it herself. "I'm not sure. Someone was here, Angie, a woman. The woman who made the call. She said she'd switched with you – that you were where she'd come from. I know it sounds crazy, and I really hope it's a dream. But this is getting scary, and I don't think we should go to this interview tomorrow. I don't care what you say. There's something strange going on here, and there are lots of jobs out there that I can get that won't put me or my cat in danger."

"Whoa! Hold on, Sam." Angie sat up so quickly Holly fell off her onto the floor. The cat stalked off in search of a more permanent place to rest. "The only place I've been in the last few minutes is asleep, and I suspect that's where you were, too. Have you ever had any sleepwalking episodes before?"

"I don't sleepwalk, Angie. I heard laughter and went to see

what was going on in here. You were gone, and it was as if you'd never been here because the sheets were gone, too. Then I saw this woman in black standing by the window holding Holly. I asked her what she wanted, and she warned me again about going on that interview tomorrow."

Angie raised a pale eyebrow. "Aha. Well, maybe you shouldn't go on that interview, after all. Maybe you should go on a vacation before you do any further job hunting."

"Are you saying I'm headed for a breakdown? I know what I saw, Angie, and it wasn't a dream or an hallucination."

"Okay." Angie gestured with her hands. "Let's say what you said actually happened, who is this mystery woman who's haunting you with threats about this Virtual Software Company? And why you? There must be hundreds of people who read that ad in Sunday's paper."

Sam had to agree with Angie. The whole thing wasn't logical. "You're right as usual, Angie. But put yourself in my shoes. What would you do under these circumstances?"

"Do you want an honest answer?"

"You'll give me one, anyway."

She smiled. "You bet I will. And you bet I'd go on that interview just to see what all the hullabaloo is all about." She looked down at Holly who'd rejoined them and was eyeing a comfortable spot on the couch on which to bed down. Angie picked up the cat and laid her on the spot. "No offense, Holly, but I'm as curious as a cat now when it comes to this interview. Even if you don't go, Sam, I will."

"I guess that settles it." Sam sat down next to Angie and petted Holly between them. "I can't let you go alone. After all, you might steal my job."

CHAPTER FOUR

—

"The best interviews—like the best biographies—should sing the strangeness and variety of the human race."

— LYNN BARBER (BRITISH JOURNALIST): *LONDON INDEPENDENT* SUNDAY, FEBRUARY 24, 1991.

S am and Angie spent the early hours of the morning talking about the anticipated interview, and then Angie brought up the topic of her wedding. Somehow, both of them ended up falling asleep on opposite sides of the couch with Holly rolled into an orange ball between them taking up the majority of the space as is typical for a feline.

A flash awakened Sam and she feared the woman in black was back, but it was Angie taking photos of Holly as she gave herself her morning grooming.

Sam yawned. "What time is it?"

"A little after eight. I've been up a while. I think we should try to get an early start. There'll probably be a crowd at this interview after the benefits that were advertised."

"That is if the job isn't gone already."

"Don't be so pessimistic. I thought you weren't interested in it anymore, anyway."

Sam stood and stretched. The morning light shining through the living room window promised a sunny day ahead, but the woman who'd stood before that window in darkness was still a part of Sam's memory. "I'm not. It's just that I hate wasting time chasing after something that will amount to nothing in either case."

Angie put down her camera. "The worst that can happen is that we satisfy our curiosities, and we get to visit your mom."

"I always like to kill two birds with one stone."

"Stop that, Sam!" Angie had gone to the kitchen and was opening a can of cat food for Holly.

"I can feed my own cat, Angie."

"That's okay. You get dressed. I'd like to catch the 9:30 out of Penn."

"I don't know what you're in a rush for."

"I have to be back by two. Mark is meeting me for lunch at the medical center's café. I spoke with him this morning before you woke up."

Sam entered the kitchen. "Those clothes look awfully wrinkled, Angie. Would you like to borrow one of my outfits?" Although Angie was proportioned much nicer than Sam was, the two women wore the same sized clothes.

Angie looked down at her wrinkled T. "Sure. I could use a hot shower, also. You go first. I'll spend some quality time with my cat niece."

After they'd showered and changed – Sam in her interview clothes, a gray tailored suit; Angie in a blue and white floral print dress that looked so much better on her than it had ever looked on Sam – they bade Holly farewell and took off to Penn Station for the train to Long Island.

It was 11:30 by the time they arrived at Virtual Software.

They'd taken the train to Hempstead and then caught a taxi to the Garden City office. When they were let off at the glass building, Angie commented wickedly, "I don't see any witches, Sam, and Halloween is another month away."

"Behave yourself, Angie. Modern-day witches aren't that easy to recognize."

"The ones in black are." She nodded at a woman in a black, hip-hugging skirt who was entering the building.

"Now I know where the term 'Black Magic' comes from. If that's my competition, I might as well leave for my mother's now."

"Oh, no you don't, Miss Stewart." Angie put her hands on Sam's shoulder nudging her forward. "We've come this far. Let's go see what this Virtual Software business is all about."

"Come into my parlor, said the spider to the fly," Sam muttered as she stepped into the revolving carousel of the building's doorway.

Virtual Software was located on the third floor of the 110 building. Sam didn't have to check any directories to know where to go because a half dozen people were murmuring about the company as they boarded the elevator, resumes and attaché cases in hand.

"Oh, boy," Angie remarked as they squeezed in among the crowd. "Looks like we've got company."

That must've been the understatement of the year. When the elevator reached the third floor, there was hardly room for the door to open, as the entire area was crammed with people.

"I knew it," Sam said. "I'm afraid you may not make your luncheon date with Mark, Angie, because we might be here a few hours before we even get in the door."

Angie smiled that mischievous smile Sam knew all too well. "That remains to be seen, my friend. Wait here. I shall return."

Before Sam could reply, Angie made her way through the crowd and toward Suite 309. She watched in disbelief as the blonde jostled and bumped along on the sea of interviewees. She could only imagine what Angie had in mind.

Less than ten minutes later, which was approximately the amount of time she thought it had taken Angie to get inside the office, Sam's name was called.

"Ms. Samantha Stewart," the unisex voice called over the roar of the crowd.

Sam stepped forward in awe. Heads turned to see who'd had the amazing luck to be admitted from the back of the line. Actually, luck wasn't the term the majority of the people had in mind when they watched her cut in front of them. Jealousy and anger flared in unemployed eyes. She heard a woman mutter in a voice meant to be heard, "I wonder whose relative she is."

Arriving at the Virtual Software suite, Sam was escorted inside by the owner of the unisex voice, a gray-haired woman in her late fifties or early sixties. "Mr. Parsons will see you now. Your photographer is in with him waiting."

Photographer? Oh, no, Sam thought. *I forgot Angie had brought along her camera. What kind of story has she concocted to get us an audience ahead of all the others?*

The gray-haired woman with the deep voice led Sam to an open door and stepped back. Sam walked into a very small but comfortable room, if that description could fit an office full of computers. Six PCs were arranged on small tables around the mahogany desk on which sat two others. A man, recognizable as Greg Parsons from his Internet photo, walked around from behind the desk to greet Sam with a sturdy handshake. Sam was too stunned to shake back. Instead, she looked over at Angie who sat, with her camera in her lap, in a black leather chair to the right of the desk.

"It's a pleasure to meet you, Ms. Stewart," Greg Parsons said, "Although our company has doubled its profits in the last year, we're still, excuse the pun, virtually unknown to the general public. Any media exposure you can give us will be greatly appreciated. Indeed, it's an honor to speak to one of *Software Review's* writers."

Sam's mouth opened, but nothing came out. Instead, Angie broke in like her ventriloquist. "It's our pleasure, Mr. Parsons. But we're aware you're very busy today, and we have our own deadlines. So once my colleague completes the interview," she glanced over at Sam, "we must be on our way."

"Of course." He pulled out a matching chair next to Angie's and beckoned Sam to take it. Then, going around his desk, he leaned back against his own chair and gave the two an appraising stare before focusing his dark eyes on Sam. "I'm ready when you are."

Sam could've died. Actually, she could've committed murder, and Angie would've been the victim. Gathering herself together and remembering her training, she decided to ask the proverbial "who," "what," "where," "when," and "why" questions of the reference interview.

"Mr. Parsons," she began, "tell me a little bit about yourself and Virtual Software. How long have you been in business, and what are your main products?"

"I'm the vice-president of Virtual Software. Like you, I come from a communications background. I was editor of *Science Journal* for five years before I became interested in telecommunications and received my master's degree in that area from MIT."

"Why did you study telecommunications?" Angie asked.

Sam would've been out of bullets had she had a gun. What was Angie doing asking questions if Sam was supposed to be the writer?

Parsons didn't seem to mind. He swiveled his chair in Angie's direction. "I wrote an article on a field of telecommunications that I became intrigued with. I wanted to know more about it."

Sam picked up the verbal ball. "Which field was that?"

"A field that deals with computer networks connecting people all over the world."

"The Internet." Sam bounced the verbal ball.

"Yes, and no." Parsons swiveled his chair in Sam's direction and steepled his hands in front of him across the desk. Sam noticed they were large hands. They'd felt strong around hers. "What I mean to say," he continued, "is that I became interested in the whole field of communications and transportation. The Internet is only one component of that field."

"Can you elaborate on that?" Angie grabbed the verbal ball and bounced it into her own court. Sam shot another imaginary bullet into her friend's head.

"It's a hard concept to explain. Let's just say I was interested in future advances that would change the present way people make contact with one another, be it by computer, telephone, or various forms of travel."

"Is that what led you to your position at a travel software company?" Sam asked.

"Perhaps."

"What about the company's founder? I hear she's missing."

Sam couldn't believe Angie would ask that. She shot a warning look toward her, but Angie was focusing her attention on Parsons, awaiting his reply.

The vice president paused, unfolding his hands. Instead of replying to Angie's question, he posed one of his own. "Did you hear about Jane's disappearance from Gerri, the editor, at *Software Review*?"

Angie nodded. "Isn't Jerry such a gossip?" Then, watching a frown spread across Parsons' brow, she added, "I'm sorry. Jerry's not a friend of yours, is he?"

In a low but deadly voice he said, "What kind of joke is this? You're not from *Software Review*, are you? If you were, you'd know Gerri Sands is a woman. And, since she happens to be a friend of mine, I'll call her right now to see if she assigned this story." He reached for the phone.

The gig was up, and Sam had the sense to admit it. "Don't bother calling, Mr. Parsons. I'm very sorry for wasting your time.

My friend was just eager to help me get an interview with you, and there were so many people waiting." She stood up, her head lowered in embarrassment. "C'mon, Angie. Mr. Parsons is busy. Let's not waste any more of his time."

Angie gathered up her camera case, but Parsons stopped her as he replaced his phone on the receiver. "Wait." He gestured toward her chair and then turned to Sam. "If you were so eager to interview for the position, I'd like to give you that chance. Miss Palmer can sit in if she wishes."

Sam remained standing. "That's very kind of you, but I really don't think you'd consider me after ..."

"On the contrary, I promise I'll give you every opportunity I've given the other applicants." He pressed a button on the phone on his desk and spoke into the intercom. "Mrs. McGee, please bring a job application into my office. Thank you."

A second later, the gray-haired woman who'd called Sam's name earlier brought in the requested form and handed it across the desk to her boss. She made no other comment and left the room after she was thanked again.

"There are a few general questions on this that I'd like you to answer, Miss Stewart. If you have a resume, I'd like to see that, also."

Sam reached into her portfolio and took out her laser-printed resume. She then went over to the desk and traded Parsons the sheet for the application.

"Take your time filling that out," he said passing her a pen before she walked back to her seat. "While you're doing that, I'd like to ask Miss Palmer a few questions."

"Me? I'm just here to accompany Sam. I don't have any of the qualifications you're seeking."

Parsons smiled, and Sam, who hadn't started answering the questionnaire, noticed a large dimple appear in his cheek. "I don't want to ask you employment questions, Miss Palmer. I'm interested in how you found out about Jane Oldsfield."

"I didn't," Angie explained. "Sam was doing some background checking on your company and read about her disappearance."

"I see." Parsons looked at Sam. "What did you think about that, Miss Stewart?"

Sam glanced down at the job application but not to read the questions. "It was interesting," she said. "I wondered why it happened and if she'd ever been found. Has she?"

"No." The single word seemed to echo in the room. "I'm currently acting president of Virtual Software, and I'm hiring someone to help me with a project Ms. Oldsfield started before she," he paused, "disappeared."

"And that involves a research and history background?"

"Correct. I'll conduct all other training."

"What happens after the new person completes the project?" Sam asked.

"They become a permanent employee."

"You said there was a lot of travel involved in the position," Angie commented from the sidelines. "Would Sam be able to bring her cat?"

Sam was about to mentally reload the gun to continuing firing imaginary bullets at her friend. Instead, she said, "That won't be a problem. You're Holly's best cat sitter, Angie."

"Is Holly your cat?" Parsons asked.

"Yes, even though she thinks she's a child."

"I had a cat," he said in a voice that carried a sad tone, as if the pet had passed away recently. Suddenly, his motivation seemed to return. "Miss Stewart, you don't need to fill out that application just yet. It can be completed once you've started the job."

Sam thought she'd missed a part of the conversation. "Job? What job?"

"The job at Virtual Software. Would you be able to start tomorrow? I'd really like Ms. Oldsfield's work to be continued as soon as possible."

"Are you sure? You haven't even looked at my resume."

"I don't need to. You've shown your research abilities through your investigation of the company, and it's a real plus that you have a cat. I like cat people."

Sam didn't know how to react. She couldn't understand why she'd been chosen out of everyone who'd applied for the job. As for the comment about the cat, was Greg Parsons serious about that? Odder things had influenced interviewers, she was sure. But did she want this job and the baggage that might go with it? A missing president and warnings that had been too close for comfort? What if she accepted the offer? As a librarian, she was used to questioning situations and looking for answers. The scenario she found herself in now didn't appear to have a quick solution, unlike a ready reference question about the diameter of the moon or the freezing temperature of water.

"I have to think it over," she said. "And I'd like to know more about my duties and the project you need me to complete."

"As I explained, most of it will involve on-the-job training. However, if you come in at this time again tomorrow, I'll provide a detailed description of the project. I'll even pay you for your time, but you have no obligation to stay if you find it's not what you had in mind."

"That sounds reasonable. I can be back here again tomorrow at," she glanced at her watch, "one o'clock."

"Terrific." Parsons stood and held out his hand to her and then Angie. "Thank you both for coming." Then he added as he turned to Sam, "Of course, I'd prefer you come alone tomorrow. This project is confidential. Even my secretary, Mrs. McGee, has no idea of the nature of the software program we'll be working on."

"Don't worry," Angie asserted, "I won't tag along again. But I did have a question about the salary. Are you really offering six figures?"

Sam almost hit her friend this time, but Parsons seemed to find the question worth answering.

"Not right away, but this project has the potential to earn the company a lot of money. I don't employ a large staff, and only my closest associates know everything that we're producing. I pay them well for that."

Before Angie could comment or ask another embarrassing question, Sam exclaimed, "I'm sure you'll fill me in on all the company policies tomorrow. But we really should be going. You're going to miss your luncheon date, Angie."

"I can keep Mark waiting a few minutes. He's always late when he makes the date. Besides, I wanted to stop in and say hi to your mom while we're out here. Now we have some good news to bring her."

Sam raised her eyebrows but didn't respond. She walked to the office door.

"Let me see you out," Parsons offered following her and placing himself between her and the exit. Seeing him out from behind the desk, she became aware of his height and muscular build. Unlike the stereotypical computer geek or bookworm, this man appeared athletic and healthy. She judged him to be nearly a foot taller than herself, which would make him approximately six-foot two. As she opened the door, he placed his arm out to hold it open and came within kissing distance of her. She looked up into a friendly but serious face with a hint of darkness she felt rather than saw. Her years of working with the public had sharpened her people instincts. She often thought that librarians should take psychology classes to learn how to deal with and understand the different type of patrons they helped.

"It's been a pleasure, Miss Stewart."

"Thank you. Sorry again about the, uh, deception."

Angie was behind Sam but kept her mouth shut.

"It was worth it. You're exactly the person I've been seeking."

"How do you know that already?" She smelled his woodsy cologne, and the scent seemed to add to his attractiveness even with the dark cloud hovering about him.

"I'm a good judge of people. You have to be in my business. See you tomorrow."

Before she could reply, he stepped out the door and headed toward his secretary's desk where a mass of angry people milled, and the telephone rang incessantly.

"Let's get out of here," Angie said, "before they see us." She referred to the mob that was ready for a lynching if they didn't get an interview. When they found out the job was already gone, it was going to get uglier.

Sam followed Angie who darted expertly through the crowds. She kept walking until they'd both taken the elevator and escaped onto the street and into the sunny day that had turned cloudy. A few sprinkles were riding the wind as they hurried to a pay phone outside the building where Angie called the taxi company that had transported them from the train station to Virtual Software. After giving their location and destination, Sam's mother's address, Angie hung up the phone. Then she inserted a few more coins and dialed another number. Sam listened as Angie apologized to Mark and asked to change their lunch date into a dinner date instead.

"You didn't have to do that," Sam told her when she was done with the call. "I know how important your time with Mark is."

"My time with my friends is important, too. Mark didn't sound too upset. He actually said he might've had to cancel on me, anyway."

"I hope you get to spend more time together when you're married."

"I doubt it, but it's okay. Quality time is what counts. C'mon, Sam, I think I see the taxi."

CHAPTER FIVE

"There's only one thing more precious than our time and that's who we spend it on."

— LEO CHRISTOPHER

On the way to Mrs. Stewart's house, Angie asked Sam what she thought of what had happened at Virtual Software that afternoon. Sam sat next to her in the back of a Long Island Yellow Taxicab. The driver, a balding man who hummed along as he listened to Bruce Springsteen tapes, started his wipers as the rain began in earnest.

"We just made it," Sam said as the heavy drops fell.

"Don't avoid my question. What do you think of your new job?"

"It's not my new job yet. I can still decline the offer."

"I noticed you making eyes at Greg."

Sam laughed. "Angie! I wasn't making eyes at him."

"Coulda fooled me. You've got to admit he's dreamy."

Bruce sang about being born in America, and the cabby had a hard time keeping the tune.

"Okay. He's nice looking, Angie. But I don't like the sound of things. I may not go back tomorrow."

Angie seemed shocked. "You have to, Sam. That's when he's going to reveal everything to you. I'm dying to know about this infamous project the missing company president was involved in. Do you think he killed her? Maybe they were lovers."

"You read too many mystery novels."

"Me?" Her mock expression of innocence was almost comical. "What about you, my dear? You're the one who sees witches at night."

"I didn't see a witch. I told you, Angie, it was a woman wearing black."

The driver had finally harmonized with Bruce as he pulled into a suburban street lined with ranch houses and green lawns. When they stopped in front of a beige house with a red Dodge parked in the driveway, Angie said, "Maybe you should've told her we were coming."

"Too late now, but at least she's home. There's her car."

The cab driver pressed a button on his tape player to rewind Bruce Springsteen's Greatest Hits and then rolled down the window separator to collect his money. "That'll be $12, ladies."

Sam handed him a ten and a five. "Keep the change."

His gap-toothed smile was wide. "Thank you. I hope you liked the music. The Boss has always been my favorite."

"Wonderful," Angie said a bit sarcastically. When they exited the cab into the no longer rainy afternoon, she whispered to Sam, "That humming drove me crazy."

Before they reached the door where a cat mat welcomed them, they saw Sam's mother standing there in a white robe.

"Girls, how good to see you," she said opening the door. "Such a pleasant surprise."

Sam felt guilty as her mother leaned out and kissed her cheek. "I don't want to come too close, dear; I have a miserable virus. The doctors still can't diagnose it. I'm afraid it might be one of those flesh-eating ones."

Sam shook her head. Ever since she could remember, her

mother had been ill with one sickness or other. But for a sickly woman, she was in ironically good health. Hypochondria was the term they used nowadays. Her father, who'd never been sick a day in his life or who never admitted to being sick a day in his life, died suddenly of a heart attack five years ago.

"I'm so sorry to hear that you're ill, Mrs. Stewart," Angie said, following Sam into the house where half a dozen or so cats came from different directions to greet them. Although the house was too dark to see any of the felines too clearly, their presence was prominently noted by the olfactory senses.

"Mom, why don't you ever keep the drapes open in here or at least turn on a light?" Sam asked.

"I don't want any peeping Tom's looking in on me, and you know how expensive electricity is today. They did without light in the dark ages, and so can I."

Sam knew she shouldn't have asked. Even in the dead of winter, her mother kept the thermostat at a cool sixty degrees. It wasn't to save on high heating costs because her father had left her mother with a comfortable life insurance premium. It was because her mother was frugal, and a frugal hypochondriac wasn't the easiest person to love.

"I think it's nice and cozy in here," Angie exclaimed. "By the way, is Jennifer around?"

Sam shrank at the mention of her younger sister's name. How her frugal mother could tolerate the company of her free-loading sister had been a mystery to her for years.

"Jenny's at school," Mrs. Stewart said. "She should be home any minute. She's taking three credits this semester, and she's also got a part-time job at the pizza parlor in the mall."

Wow, Sam thought. Aloud she said to her mother, "I didn't know Jen had gone back to school again. What's she studying now?"

Mrs. Stewart paused, then put a hand to her Lady Clairol Ash Blonde hair in dire need of a touchup. "She's taking science, I think; a class called psychic phenomenon. It sounds very interesting."

"I bet. What are they studying; the X Files?"

"Now, Sam," Angie interjected. "Psychic phenomenon is a very serious subject these days."

Sam shrugged her shoulders and tried to change the subject. "Mother, what have you been doing besides going to the doctor?"

"Sam, that isn't nice." Angie stuck up for Mrs. Stewart.

"Don't mind, Sammy. I know she means well but has a hard time showing it."

"I do mean well," Sam said, "and I mean exactly what I say. You spend so much time with Dr. Carter that I bet the town gossips think you're having an affair with him."

"I don't go to the doctor unless I have to which, unfortunately, has been too often. Now, girls, if you don't mind, I feel a touch of my virus acting up and would like to lie down. Feel free to take anything from the refrigerator except a piece of the Entenmann cake. It wasn't on sale today, and I'm saving it for company."

"But we are company," Sam said.

"No," Angie defended Mrs. Stewart again. "We're family."

The older woman smiled. "That's right, and I think of you as my third daughter, Angie." As she made her way toward the back of the house, a few cats followed her robe trying to catch a few of the white threads hanging from the hem.

"You should be ashamed of yourself," Angie said when Mrs. Stewart was out of earshot.

"Me? You're the one who's so family-starved that you'd adopt such a dysfunctional one as mine." She was sorry she'd said the words as soon as they were out of her mouth. "I'm sorry, Angie, I didn't mean that. It's just that she's so frustrating. You only see her when you visit with me. I spent twenty-three years living with her."

Angie was about to respond with what Sam believed would be a retort when a sports car pulled up next to the Dodge in the driveway. Jennifer Stewart was home from her Psychic Phenomenon class.

Jennifer was a younger version of Mrs. Stewart in appearance. Her blonde hair was also a product of the bottle, and she had her mother's same high cheekbones and narrow features. Sam, on the other hand, had taken after her father with the rounder, softer features some found more appealing.

"Hello, Big Sister," Jennifer said, entering the house. "Has the prodigal daughter returned?"

"Just visiting," Sam replied. "Angie and I had something to do on the Island today, so we thought we'd drop by."

"Sam went on a job interview, and they hired her," Angie pointed out.

Sam began loading the imaginary gun.

"How interesting," Jennifer said, flopping herself down on the cat-clawed sofa in the living room. "Tell me about it, Sis."

Angie sat next to Jennifer, but Sam remained standing. "There's nothing to tell yet. The job is with a software company in Garden City doing research work."

"Sounds fascinating." Why did Jennifer's voice always have that sarcastic tone? "I'm doing a lot of research for the class I'm taking in psychic phenomenon. Do you know that you're most likely to receive psychic impulses in your sleeping state?"

"Hey," Angie exclaimed, "Maybe that's what happened to you, Sam."

Now Sam had to sit down. She chose the ugly, puke-green chair across from the sofa that her mother's cats had used as a substitute scratching post.

"Did you have a psychic experience, Sam?" Her sister feigned interest when Sam knew the only thing her sister was interested in was herself.

"No. My experience was real. Someone broke into my apartment last night while Angie was staying over. Angie didn't see her, but I did."

Sam was glad that Angie made no further comments on the subject and that Jennifer returned to her own self-absorbed musings.

"I really love this class, Sam. I've learned so much about the paranormal."

"Sounds like a psych course I took in my undergraduate days. But what do you plan to do with it?"

"I don't know. I'm sure I'll be able to fit it into my career plans somehow."

"If you want an older sister's advice, not that I think you do, but most people decide on their career path and fit classes to it rather than the other way around."

"I know, but my major is now interdisciplinary."

"What does that mean?" Angie inquired.

"It means a little bit of everything."

"Or a lot of nothing," Sam ventured.

"Not necessarily. Most employers prefer a well-rounded employee."

"That's true, but on the scale of well-roundedness, you're a bit overly plump." Sam didn't want to bring up the previous dozen or so career fields her younger sister had explored and found wanting. The term "perpetual student" fit Jennifer Stewart like a glove. At twenty-five she still hadn't earned a degree in anything but had accumulated more credits than some doctorate programs required.

It was just as well that Jennifer shook her bleached locks and changed the subject to one Sam dreaded more, their mother. "Where is mother?" she asked.

"Resting. She thinks she has a flesh-eating virus."

Jennifer smiled. "Last week, it was Lyme Disease even though she never goes out of the house unless it's to the doctors."

Finally, they were on a subject they agreed upon. Unfortunately, Angie wouldn't let them attack Mrs. Stewart and share whatever sibling bonding was possible between them.

"I don't think it's right to talk about your mother that way. What if she really is ill?"

"If mother stops complaining about her health, then we'll know we have something to worry about," Jennifer said.

"Anyway," Sam put in, tiring of a topic that was literally tiring, "We really should be going now. Angie already cancelled one date with her fiancée. I don't want her to have to cancel another."

"How is Mark?" Jennifer asked. She'd met him once when he'd visited with Angie for her mother's annual Christmas party. At this festive event, Mrs. Stewart opens her hearth and home to all family and friends who don't mind her walking around blowing her nose with a Santa Claus handkerchief telling them not to help her even though she has the flu.

"He's great," Angie replied. "That's why I'm marrying him. I can't believe the date is only six weeks away."

"It must be a wonderful feeling. Personally, I wouldn't know," Jennifer said. She didn't elaborate on her response because both Sam and Angie knew that Jennifer planned to spend her life single. She'd had her share of boyfriends but dropped each one who tried to get serious. Basically, she was too lazy to deal with taking care of someone else while she wasn't doing such a hot job of taking care of herself. Sam only hoped she'd pick up enough survival skills to exist in the world after their mother was gone. If not, Sam wasn't prepared to take her in for the measly rent her mother accepted.

"Sam's right, we'd better get going," Angie relented. "Say goodbye to your mother for us. I hope she feels better, or at least thinks she feels better."

"Sure thing. And if I don't see you before the wedding, give my regards to Dr. Mark."

"Will do."

They were at the front door, which Sam had opened to let in the now sunny rays. One of her mother's cats was curled up asleep on the welcome mat.

"Good luck with your studies," Sam told her sister.

"Thanks." Jennifer sounded genuinely appreciative. "And good luck on your new job, too." She opened the latch to the screen door and let in the black and white cat. "Oh, Sis ..."

Sam turned.

"Do you need me to call a cab or anything?"

"No. We can walk to the station from here, but thanks for asking."

Angie was quiet on the walk to the train. When she spoke halfway there, she sounded sad. Sam wondered if she thought of her sister whom she'd never had the opportunity to grow up with.

"Jennifer loves you a lot," she said.

"I guess, but not more than she loves herself."

"What's wrong with that?"

"Don't get philosophical on me, Angie."

They were at the train station with the setting sun in their eyes. If a stranger came upon them standing side by side, he or she would describe the two women as attractive ladies in their late twenties to early thirties dressed in business clothes, perhaps returning from their job in the city on the 5:15 commuter train, only they were headed in the opposite direction from the suburbs to the city.

Angie didn't answer. Instead, she unzipped her camera case and began taking pictures of the crowd waiting for the train, the ticket booth, the sun, and the rails. Sam knew the eyepiece obscured her friend's tears.

CHAPTER SIX

"Time with cats is never wasted."

— COLETTE

A ngie remained silent on the ride back to Manhattan. She'd stopped taking photos after she'd boarded the train but sat near the window looking away from Sam.

"I'm sorry," Sam finally said before they'd reached Penn Station.

Angie turned to face her with wet eyes. "It's not your fault, Sam. It's just that whenever I'm reminded of my family, I keep remembering the night I lost them all."

Sam reached out and touched her friend's arm. "It's okay, Angie. You have Mark now. You can start your own family."

Angie laughed, but there was a break in her voice. "Can you imagine all the baby pictures we'll have?"

"If all the shots you've taken of my cat are any indication, you'd better hope you get plenty of photo albums for wedding presents."

· · ·

Sam invited Angie to stop by her apartment before she headed to meet Mark at St. Luke's, but she refused. "Sorry, Sam. I'd rather get back to my place now unless you're still nervous about last night and need someone to come home with you."

"I think I've gotten over that, but I hope I did the right thing about this job. You go ahead, Angie. The only thing I have to fear at the apartment is a hungry cat, and since you don't have one, you don't realize how scary that can be."

Angie laughed again, but she seemed brighter this time. "Well, call me if you have any other problems besides a spoiled feline, and don't forget to let me know how everything goes tomorrow."

"I won't, and thanks for today."

"For accompanying you on the interview and getting you in ahead of everybody else? That's the least a friend can do."

"I'm not talking about that." They were walking toward Sam's apartment uptown. It had turned warm, but even this early in the season she could see a few leaves changing color on the trees. "I meant thanks for encouraging me to visit Mom and Jennifer. I piss and moan about them a lot, but they're my family as dysfunctional as they are."

"And I'm your friend as dysfunctional as I am."

Sam tapped Angie on her shoulder. "I almost forgot you're wearing my dress."

"I'll wash it and bring it back to you, but with your six-figure salary you'll be able to buy plenty more."

"I won't be making six figures right away, even if I do take the job after tomorrow," Sam reminded her.

"Just remember your poor starving artist friend when you do start rolling in the bucks."

They had one more block to go before Sam's building. "You're far from starving, Angie. In fact, between you and Mark, you probably make six figures."

"Yes, but Mark owes a medical school loan, and I have a wedding to pay for."

Sam nodded. "I won't forget you, Angie. I promise." She opened her purse and took out the key for her apartment. "We're here. Give my regards to Dr. Mark, as my sister calls him."

"I will. Call me tomorrow." Angie watched Sam enter the apartment complex before she turned to continue her walk back to her own apartment a few blocks away.

As Sam walked up the stairs, she ran into Mr. Clancy from across the hall. John Clancy was an 80-year-old widower who walked with a cane. He spent most of his days watching television in his apartment or sitting on a bench in Washington Square Park feeding the birds. Since she'd met him when she moved into her apartment nine years ago, Mr. Clancy had been a kind and dear friend. He told her she reminded him of his granddaughter who lived in California and sent him letters each week. She often checked on him to see if he needed anything, especially company. He seemed to need a lot of that and enjoyed telling her his old World War II tales or stories about his kids and their kids whose photos lined his apartment but who didn't seem to exist outside their frames because he seldom had visitors.

"Good day, Sammy," he said, speaking down to her as he negotiated the stairs. Sam often wondered why he'd chosen an apartment on the second level when he had problems walking.

"Hello, John. Do you need any help getting down?"

"Of course not." He smiled displaying teeth that were only slightly stained from the cigars he gave up smoking six months ago, not for health reasons but because he wanted to prove he could do it. He'd bet Sam a dinner out at a restaurant if he could quit cold turkey, and she ended up treating him to prime rib at Tavern on the Green.

"Where are you going?" she asked as he made his way slowly down the steps two feet and one stick at a time. She stopped by the side of the rail to allow him room to descend.

"Over to the market to pick up some food for dinner. Need anything?"

Sam almost felt guilty about not offering to do his shopping that week, but he preferred to be independent, and she knew it was better psychologically if not also physically for an older person to do as much as they could for themselves. "No, thanks. But if you'd like to join me for dinner tomorrow night, I'll make your favorite, spaghetti and meatballs. We can celebrate my new job."

Mr. Clancy's small blue eyes lit up behind his thick lenses. He'd had a glaucoma operation a few years ago, which had helped his sight to a degree, but he still needed to wear a strong prescription. "That sounds wonderful. And, congratulations, you must tell me all about it."

"I certainly will. Is five tomorrow night, okay?" She knew Mr. Clancy liked to eat early, and she was pretty sure she'd be back from the post-interview by that time. She had to admit to herself that she'd invited the old man as much for her benefit as for his.

"Fine. Oh, and Sammy." He was almost at the bottom step. She looked down at him.

"Yes?"

"I'm not complaining, even though you know how I feel about cats. They're too sneaky for me. Yours has never given me a problem, but today it howled. I never heard such a racket."

"Oh, my gosh!" Sam was alarmed. Holly was probably hungrier than she expected, even though she'd left out dry food. Either that or she'd hurt herself in some way. Holly hardly cried unless Sam was home, and she wanted her attention. "I'm sorry about that, John. I'll take care of her."

Sam raced up the last few steps to her door to see what was wrong with Holly. A fear, akin to one a mother feels for her child when it could be in danger, flooded through her. Her hands fumbled with the key as she turned it in the lock. "Holly," she called out even before she'd switched on her light. Even before she noticed another shape in the room. Even before she heard the unfamiliar yowl and saw the unfamiliar yellow eyes. Even before she realized there was another cat in her apartment.

"What in the world are you doing here?" Sam asked the large gray and white cat that sat in the middle of her living room. "And where is Holly?"

As if in answer to her "mother's" question, the orange tabby lifted up the bottom tapestry flap of the couch and revealed her head. She was clearly on the defensive from the intruding cat.

Sam couldn't understand how the other animal had gotten into her apartment. Her door had been locked, as had all her windows. She always rechecked them before leaving to make sure Holly couldn't escape. And yet, here was the little critter, or rather the large critter, who must've been twice Holly's size.

"Miarrr," the cat cried. Knowing that the feline language consisted of dozens of sounds that stood for various commands and comments from "I'm hungry," to "let me out," Sam tried to decipher this kitty's request.

"Hey, big fella, what do you want?"

"MIARRR!" The golden eyes were huge. Holly ducked back underneath the couch.

"I'm sorry. I can't understand you. I'm used to little girl cat language, and you're a big Tom."

The cat stopped crying but looked up at her with a strange expression. He looked as if he was lost and was trying to figure out where he was.

"Maybe you want some food." Sam went to her kitchen and opened up a can of Holly's cat food for the newcomer. Even though the cat looked as if it was well fed, she thought she'd be able to entice Holly out from her hiding place with the aroma of Whiska's Lamb and Rice. As the new cat lowered its gray head to eat from the bowl, an orange streak of fur flashed into the kitchen writhing and hissing at the beast that had invaded her territory. Holly looked comical with her tail inflated into an orange and white striped brush. Sam laughed at her. The other cat backed slowly out of the way and let the resident cat eat first.

Sam was so preoccupied watching the two animals that she was unnerved by the sound of her phone ringing. As she went to answer it, she couldn't help but fear it was the "lady in black" calling with another warning. After all, Sam had, for all intent and purpose, accepted the job she'd been warned not to interview for.

Sam's fears were alleviated when the voice on the other end was male, but then she had other worries when she realized it was Peter Clark.

"Sam," he said after her pensive "hello." "It's me, Peter. I just called to see how you're doing. You don't sound too good. Are you okay?"

She fought to regain her composure, and her pride was there to help. "Fine, Peter. What do you really want?"

There was a pause, as Peter Perfect contemplated his next move. "I told you. I wanted to make sure you were okay. I miss you, Sam. I was such an idiot, and I'm sorry. I know I've apologized before, but I'm hoping you've had some time to think about it and will accept my apology now." The words sounded false. They could've been read off a soap opera cue card.

Sam recalled the dozens of apologies Peter had offered following their breakup, some of which included roses or stuffed teddy bears. She'd almost given in several times but had forced herself to be strong. Angie had warned her that men like Peter never stopped fooling around, despite their bad feelings afterward.

"Listen, I'm really busy right now, Peter," she said firmly, "We've been through all of this before. You're a great guy, but I need someone more loyal. Don't call me again, or I'll call the police."

There was no reply from the other end, only the short click of the receiver being hung up. Sam knew Peter wasn't the type to stalk or harass a woman, so she knew she had nothing to fear on that level. On the other hand, she wondered about the threat she'd received regarding Virtual Software. Could Peter have found out about her interview with the company somehow? Could he have asked one of his female friends to make that warning call and midnight appearance in her apartment? But why?

Before Sam could give that train of thought much consideration, she found herself turning back to the cats to see how they were mingling and if they needed more food. But when she looked back by the cat dish, Holly was the only one there.

"Mr. Gray cat," she called. "Where did you go?"

Sam went through the apartment, looking for the mystery cat who seemed to have disappeared as unexpectedly as he'd appeared. The only trace of the animal seemed to be some gray fur that had fallen off it probably during a confrontation with Holly. As Sam picked up the small pieces of fur from the living room carpet and began rolling them into a ball, she heard laughter echo through her apartment. She felt like Holly a few minutes ago when her fur had stood up on end. She'd heard that sound before, and it chilled her.

She knew she should've run to her phone and dialed 911. Instead, she followed the sound toward her bedroom. "Who's there?" she called out stupidly. She wasn't looking for a reply. She only wanted to alert the woman that she'd heard her.

At the entrance to her room, she paused. The lights were on, even though she'd turned them off when she'd left that morning. The last time she'd seen the lady in black, it had been in darkness late at night. Now there were no shadows to obscure the woman's face as she smiled at Sam from where she lay sprawled across the bed. Sam nearly fainted as she realized where she'd seen the woman before. The Internet hadn't done her justice. She was even lovelier than her photo with long dark hair and ivory skin that came wrapped in a shapely package. She still wore black, but there were pearls at her throat and wrists.

CHAPTER SEVEN

"All Right," said the [Cheshire] Cat; and this time it vanished quite slowly, beginning with the end of the tail, and ending with the grin, which remained some time after the rest of it had gone."

— LEWIS CARROLL: "ALICE'S ADVENTURE'S IN
WONDERLAND"

"Jane Oldsfield," Sam said in a voice that held no greeting.

"In the flesh, my dear," the woman replied, sitting up and dangling her long legs over Sam's quilted bedspread.

"What do you want?"

Jane shook her hair back. "I already told you that, but you didn't listen."

"If it's about the job, I won't be going tomorrow. It isn't worth it."

The woman laughed again, but it was a shortened version of her usual cacophony. "Oh, you'll go, Samantha, but you won't be working for Greg. You'll be working for me."

Sam took a step backward. Whatever this woman, who was supposedly missing had up her sleeve, she didn't want to know about it. She had to get to the phone and call the police, as she should've done when the woman first invaded her home.

As if reading her mind, the woman said in a voice as slick as oil, "Don't do anything silly like calling the police because when they arrive, they won't find me here. It would make you look foolish. I would rather avoid that. In fact, if you cooperate, you'll find I'm a decent boss to work for. So, let's go into the kitchen, have some tea, and I'll fill you in on everything." Sam knew she couldn't trust this woman, but something told her to play along with whatever she suggested. "Okay, but you'd better make this fast because my friend is coming over in a few minutes," she lied.

"Do you mean Angie?" the woman smiled again baring lips painted a dark shade of red. "She's with Mark right now having dinner. They're getting married in November, aren't they?"

"How do you know all this?"

As if she lived there instead of visiting only twice, Jane Oldsfield prepared tea in Sam's kitchen while Sam watched in a dreamlike state. Was she actually dreaming? Angie had suggested that was the case the first time, but Sam knew that if she pinched herself, the pain would be real.

"Do you take milk or sugar in this?" Jane asked as if they were old friends getting together for a tea-time chat. "No, don't tell me. You use just a drop of milk." She walked to the refrigerator and took out the open half quart. Holly ran in, as she always did when milk was poured. When she saw the strange woman, she stopped in the doorway. Jane knelt down and called to the cat, "Here, Holly. I won't bite. Unlike Floppy, I won't scratch either."

"Is Floppy your cat?" Sam asked, wondering what the correlation was between the gray cat that had disappeared when she found Jane laughing in her bedroom and the woman who'd nonchalantly invaded her kitchen and her life.

"My cat? No. He belongs to Greg. At least, he used to belong to Greg. He's sort of mine right now. You could say he works for me. In fact, you and he will have a lot in common if you agree to my plan."

Sam was angry. This woman had a lot of nerve breaking into her apartment and then acting as if she owned the place. "Well, when are you going to tell me this big secret, anyway?" she asked in a voice she tried to keep level.

Jane stepped away from the cat who was keeping her distance from the intruder. Picking up the teacups, she brought them over to the table and sat down across from Sam. In a low voice, even steadier than the one Sam had tried to adopt, she said, "This isn't going to be easy to understand at first, Sam. I know you'll have a lot of questions when I'm through with the story, but I may not be able to answer them all. I don't expect that you trust me, but it doesn't really matter. If you don't join my team, someone else will."

"Team? Who else is there?" Sam asked, avoiding her tea for fear it was poisoned.

"Just Floppy and me right now. That's what makes this so exciting. The cat won't need any of our profits, so you and I can split everything fifty-fifty." She smiled, parting her red lips. "If you think Greg's offer of a six-figure income is appealing, you'll love my offer even more. How do millions sound? Maybe billions. People will pay a lot of money for the service we'll be able to provide once the project is completed." She stirred her tea with one of Sam's spoons. Then she reached into her pocket and took out the round object Sam had seen her use once before. Close up, it resembled a compass. It had markings on it to indicate direction but also other strange markings that looked like foreign letters or symbols of some type. Jane placed the object between them on the table. "All you have to do is place six of these in the right place at the right time in the right year. I've already placed two. I'm getting close to placing the third. When all twelve are placed, the world will be ready for bidding on the ultimate travel software package."

Sam put her hand out but was afraid to touch the compass-like device. She noticed that it was lit from within – a blue glow that grew from its center and spread to its circumference in an alternating rhythm of light. "What is it?"

"A work of art. A very advanced microchip housed in a protective sphere. There's a technical term, but I won't bore you with it. Let's just say it's a time-travel computer. I invented it, and I'm going to sell it once it's perfected." She reached out, took the round orb, and turned it gently in her right palm. "No one, especially not Greg Parsons, is going to stop me."

Sam feared the woman who sat within inches of her was insane. There was no logical explanation to what she was saying. If only Sam could get to the phone and call the police.

"You don't believe me?" The woman put down what she contended was a time-travel computer. "I could show you a demonstration, but I don't think you're quite ready for that. You need training. Greg thinks he can train you, but he wasn't the one who invented the TTDs — that's what I'm calling them for now: The Time-Travel Disks. He could've been my partner, but he chose to disagree with me about the benefits of the project. The trouble is, he's too ethical. I used to think he was more progressive than that. When we went to school together, he touted the new technology." She paused for a sip of tea. "But why should I bother you with my past man troubles? I promised I'd fill you in on all the details, and I will. Not all of it will make sense until you see for yourself, but the main decision you have to make is which one of us you're going to work for. You see, Sam, dear, you're going to work for one of us. According to the future view, you choose Greg because he's the good guy. I want to change that, and I have the power to do so. If you decide to go along with Greg, I can do some very nasty things to you. Talk about threats. How would you like it if you were never born? If I can find the right polarized points on this gadget," she held up the time-travel disk, "I can prevent your parents from ever meeting. Of course, I can also do that to Greg. He fears me, but not as much as he should."

Sam tried to comprehend what she was hearing, but all she could concentrate on was getting help before this mad woman took out a gun from another pocket and shot her.

As Sam was planning to make a run for her door, Mr. Clancy called from the hall. "Sammy, I picked up some vegetables for you at the market. Fresh zucchini and tomatoes. If you like, I can use them to make up the sauce for tomorrow night. Sammy? Are you there?" A few taps from his cane followed the question.

"Rats!" Jane exclaimed. "I'd better go. I'll be back again, Sam. In the meantime, talk to Greg tomorrow. Maybe he can save me some of the work by filling you in on things. But think about what I said. I can be a great ally but an even greater enemy." She picked up what she'd referred to as both a time-travel disk and a time-travel computer and punched a few of the tiny keys on the round object. In less than a second, Jane Oldsfield was gone. Her unoccupied chair stood a few inches from the table. Sam looked around the room to make sure the woman hadn't hidden somewhere despite the fact that she'd been staring right at her when she literally vanished into thin air. There didn't seem to be any rational justification for what Sam had witnessed. It was either a very sophisticated magic trick on par with those carnival and circus disappearing acts or a realistic version of a "Beam me up, Scotty" episode from the original Star Trek.

"Sammy, are you okay?" Clancy called, his rappings quicker and louder.

On wobbly legs, Sam answered the door. As she opened it, she tried to compose herself for the old man's sake. There was no sense in frightening him, but for his own safety, she would have to send him back to his apartment as soon as possible. Then she'd call the police and tell them her crazy story or at least the portions of it they could do something about and would believe.

"Sorry, John," she said. "I was on the phone."

The old man looked relieved but not totally satisfied with her excuse. "I didn't mean to disturb you, but I wanted to bring these over," he said indicating the brown grocery bag he held in his arms.

"I'll take that, and don't worry about the sauce. I invited you tomorrow night, so I'll do all the cooking. I appreciate the vegetables. That was thoughtful." She took the bag from him, but her neighbor walked in, anyway.

"Least I could do. How's your cat, Sammy? She seems to have quieted down."

In all the commotion, Sam had forgotten about Holly. But, at the mention of her, she came out from where she was hiding under the couch. Sam bent down and petted her head as Holly circled her legs sniffing at the familiar Sam scent and probably wondering where the bad woman with the fat cat had gone.

Mr. Clancy avoided the tabby and made himself comfortable on the couch. He glanced around the room at the photos of Holly in various positions and activities. "How is your friend, the photographer, doing these days?" he asked as Sam went to the kitchen to put away the vegetables. "She's getting married soon, isn't she?"

"Beginning of November," Sam replied not really up to small talk. If she encouraged him, she knew the lonely man would stay hours. She couldn't allow that with a possibly dangerous woman who could drop in or out and make herself as well as others disappear whenever she wanted to.

"I hate to be rude, John, but I'm expecting some company soon."

The old man smiled, and the deep wrinkles at the corner of his eyes became even more pronounced. "Did you make up with Peter?"

"No, and I never will."

His smile remained fixed. "Good for you. Who's the new fella?"

Sam didn't want to take this train of conversation to any

further stops. "Please, John, I really need you to leave now. I'll see you tomorrow night. Thanks again for the vegetables."

"I get the picture." The old man got up, stiffly leaning onto his cane. "My granddaughter may be calling me in a few minutes, anyhow."

Why were old people so good at planting seeds of guilt? Sam had too many things on her mind right now to fall into that old trap. She followed Clancy to the door. "Give Betsy my regards," she said.

Realizing Sam meant business, he nodded and stepped out of the apartment. As soon as he was gone, Sam bolted the door even though she knew that would offer no protection against a time traveler. Then she ran to the phone and dialed "911." After giving her address and the fact that someone had broken into her apartment, Sam waited for the police to arrive. Luckily, she didn't have a repeat visit from Jane Oldsfield.

Two police officers arrived at her apartment within fifteen minutes. One was a tall young cop with dark hair and a moustache whom she might have contemplated flirting with if she hadn't been so upset or hadn't noticed the gold band on the fourth finger of his left hand. The other was an older man with a sparse amount of graying hair and a potbelly that hung below the blue folds of his uniform.

The younger man spoke first when she answered their knock. "What's the problem, ma'am?"

"Someone broke into my apartment last night and this afternoon. The same woman. I know who she is, but I've never met her before."

The younger man must have taken her strange words for hysterics. "Why don't you let us in and have a seat, and we'll go over everything with you," he suggested.

"No. Wait, Rod," the older cop said. "We have to check the door locks and the windows for forcible entry, although I doubt anyone would've used the windows at this height." He started examining the front door, but Sam stopped him.

"You won't find forcible entry," she told him mimicking his police jargon. "She didn't break in."

"Hold on a minute," the officer named Rod said flipping open a notepad and getting ready to jot down Sam's answers. "You just told us the perpetrator broke into your apartment twice."

Sam was stymied. How could she explain that Jane Oldsfield hadn't used the windows or the door? "Uh, well, I meant, I must've left the door open. But she was trespassing."

"Aha," Rod was scribbling some notes. "You actually saw this woman? What did she say when you caught her in your apartment?"

This was the real test. Sam wished she'd rehearsed her lines. She wasn't too good at improvising, so she decided to tell as much of the truth as she could without being considered a kook. "Yes, Officer, I did see the, uh, perpetrator. I recognized her from a photo I saw on the Internet when I was doing research for a job interview."

The older officer raised his bushy gray eyebrows that were thicker than any of the hairs on his head. "All this technology stuff is getting out of hand. The Internet is just another avenue for crime if you ask me. Continue, Miss. Who is this mystery computer lady supposed to be?"

"Harry," the younger cop said tapping his pad with the tip of his pencil for emphasis, "The perpetrator may have nothing to do with computers. Plenty of people are on the Internet today with their own web pages and everything."

"Don't get techie on me, Rod. Just let the young lady finish her story." He strode into the room and plopped down on the sofa in the same spot John Clancy had occupied earlier. Sam made the comparison and realized the policeman was probably only about a decade younger than her neighbor.

"Sure." Rod remained standing, but he moved into the living

room. "You can sit, too, Miss. Please. It must've been quite a shock coming home to find a stranger in your apartment. Although, you did say she also trespassed last night. Can you explain that?"

The younger officer's avoidance of the term "break in" on her account, made Sam more comfortable. She took a seat on the opposite end of the couch from the officer Harry and faced Rod. Before she could reply to any of the questions they'd posed her, Harry exclaimed, "Just a sec, Rod. I want to hear about this job she was researching. Tell us about that, Miss. The job you were checking on the Internet."

Sam suddenly felt as if she was being interrogated. "Excuse me, Officers, but I can only answer one question at a time. Let me tell you the story from the beginning and then you can ask whatever else I haven't answered. Okay?"

The policemen nodded like little boys who'd tried to see how far they could get before being disciplined.

Sam followed with a pretty accurate account of the previous night's experience and that of the last few hours. She even threw in the time travel references but defended them by saying that they were obviously the rantings of a mad woman. When she was done telling her tale, Rod spoke first.

"We'll have to check with the Nassau County Police, Harry, and find out who's in charge of the Jane Oldsfield case." He looked back at Sam. "I don't know how you feel about going on that interview tomorrow, but our main concern is your safety. Unfortunately, we won't be able to put any guards on this apartment because there was nothing taken, and no physical harm done to anyone. On the other hand, if you hear from or see this Oldsfield woman again, if that is who she is, call the police immediately."

"Is that all you can do?"

"Afraid so," Harry replied getting up from the couch with a huff. "Just make sure your door is locked and bolted. Of course, if Jane Oldsfield really can travel through space and time, that won't help."

"Don't mock her, Harry. This woman sounds dangerous. There must be some reason she doesn't want Miss Stewart to take that job." Rod put his pad away and extended his hand to Sam. "Once I find out who's handling the Oldsfield case on Long Island, I'll let you know, or have him get in touch with you. If this really is Virtual Software's missing president, she's going to have some explaining to do. In either case, be careful."

"Thank you," Sam said, shaking first his hand and then his partner's. "But would you advise me to go on that interview tomorrow or not?"

"Wait and see," the young cop said. "As soon as you hear from us or the detective from Nassau, we should have a better handle on this, and that'll determine how you should proceed."

"I hope so," Sam said. "I'll lock my doors. Just in case."

Rod winked at her. "Goodnight then.

CHAPTER EIGHT

"There is one kind of robber whom the law does not strike at,
and who steals what is most precious to men: time."

— NAPOLEON I

After the officers left, Sam tried to settle down with a novel
she'd been reading to keep her mind off things, but her
thoughts kept returning to what had transpired between her and
Jane Oldsfield and what might happen at tomorrow's interview
if she decided to go. After flipping through a dozen pages and
realizing she wasn't getting any further than the one line she was
reading over and over again, Sam knocked Holly gently but
firmly off her lap and got off the couch.

Heading for the kitchen, she paused before she entered the
room to make sure no one was sitting in the seat Jane had
previously occupied. But the chair was still in the same place, a
few inches from the table as if someone had pushed it out to
slide behind it. The teacups were also there, and Sam noticed
hers was still full, cold no doubt by now, and the other was
almost empty except for a few drops at the bottom and some
dark dregs of tea leaves. She cleared the table and rinsed out

the teacups in the sink. She kept thinking that maybe she should've left the other cup for evidence, but the police were emphatic about the fact that no crime had taken place besides trespassing and that couldn't actually be proved in light of the fact that she had left her door unlocked, a stupid and dangerous thing to do in New York City. A favorite phrase of her mother's came back to her suddenly, "if you invite trouble, don't be surprised if it visits" – a takeoff on some famous quote, probably, but actually pretty true. Only she hadn't left her apartment door open, but the police wouldn't have believed her story otherwise.

Sam felt too fidgety to consider lying down, let alone sleeping that night. Instead, she went to her cupboard and took out a box of Snackwells chocolate chip cookies. The label read "50 percent less fat" than the leading chocolate chip cookies. *Yeah, well we'll see about that. If you eat the whole box, does that mean you gain 50 percent less pounds?* Sam took the box with her and returned to the living room. Holly was back on the couch but gave her a hostile look when she approached as if to say, "Don't think you're comfying up with me again after knocking me off your lap." Sam didn't have the heart, or the nerve, to disturb her again, so she settled herself on the opposite side of the couch next to her tapestry cat pillow and used the remote to flip on the television.

While she was digging into the box for a handful of the cookies as the ten o'clock news was about to come on, the phone rang. "Damn it," Sam exclaimed, and her cat's ears flattened at the indignity of the remark. "I wasn't addressing you," Sam said feeling perfectly comfortable talking to the animal. After all, if she could speak with a time traveler, talking to a cat was nothing.

She walked back to the kitchen and picked up the phone. "Hello." She prayed it wasn't Jane.

The voice on the other end was gruff and unfamiliar. "Ms. Stewart?"

"Yes?" The next worst bet after the lady in black would be a telephone solicitor.

"This is Detective Montmart from the Old Brookville Police on Long Island. I was told you have some information regarding the whereabouts of Miss Jane Oldsfield."

That would've been her third choice for worst phone call, tying with another call from Peter. "I don't know her whereabouts at this time, but she was in my apartment this afternoon. Did Rod and Harry, I mean, the Manhattan police, contact you?"

"Yes, they did. They said Ms. Oldsfield was trespassing in your apartment and told you some weird story about time travel."

Sam tried to visualize the man on the other end of the line. What she came up with was a mix between Officer Harry and John Clancy subtracting another decade or so from the policeman. Mix and match the potato heads. His last name sounded French, but the voice had no accent except a North Shore Long Island one. *Rich cop,* she thought, *probably deals with a lot of Gold Coast burglaries.*

"Yes," she replied. "That's correct. I thought she was crazy. I was afraid she had a gun or another weapon with her."

"Do you know why she may have visited you, Miss Stewart?"

Because I invited trouble. "I think it had to do with the job interview I went on this afternoon for the company she's president of."

"Virtual Software?"

"Yes. Look, Detective Montmart, how can I be of assistance to you?"

"I was going to pose the same question to you." He coughed, and she thought it sounded like a smoker's cough – it would explain the gruff voice. "Excuse me. What I wanted to propose, Miss Stewart, was that we meet and discuss this. As you're aware, Miss Oldsfield has been missing since July. I've been assigned to her case and have noticed some unusual things going on at her house. If she's in the area, I'd like to know what she's been up to. What I'd like to suggest is that you go to that meeting tomorrow, ask Mr. Parsons some questions, and find out exactly what he's planning. I have a feeling he may be in on this, too."

Sam didn't like the sound of this. The guinea pig usually doesn't like the lay out of the maze. "Will I have any protection?"

"I'll be there in an unmarked car. In fact, I'd like to speak with you before the meeting. What time is it?"

"Parsons said around the same as the interview time. We agreed 1 pm. "

"Why don't we arrange to meet around twelve? There's a diner on Hempstead Turnpike not far from Virtual Software. It's called the Turnpike Diner. There's a small strip mall near there. Do you know the place?"

"I ate there once with my sister."

"Good. Meet me there at noon. I won't be in uniform. Look in the smoking section for the gray-haired guy with the scar on his cheek. I know that sounds like something out of a detective story, but it didn't happen on the job. One of my dogs did it. I raise pit bulls."

"*Oh, wonderful,*" Sam thought, mentally drawing a long white gash on the cheek of a younger officer Harry/John Clancy and putting a Marlborough in his mouth. "All right. I'll see you then, Detective Montmart."

There was no goodbye. Just a click. Sam stood there with the phone's receiver in her hand feeling a wave of apprehension wash over her. She knew she'd never get to sleep now. Returning to the sofa and her cookies, she went on her eating binge as the news flashed its normal murders, accidents, and disasters by her. When she was down to her last crumb, she didn't feel any calmer but now had an upset stomach. "Oh, Holly, you're so lucky," she told the cat who was sleeping on the other end of the couch. "You don't have a worry in the world." Then she thought of the gray cat that had supposedly belonged to Greg Parsons. What had Jane Oldsfield meant when she said the animal worked for her? There were so many unanswered questions, and Sam wasn't sure she wanted the answers to all of them. However, she didn't know if she was going to have a choice. If Jane Oldsfield was sane and this wasn't part of a very long bad dream or hallucination, then what trouble had she invited into her life this time?

She tossed the empty cookie box onto the floor and lay back against the cushion. Closing her eyes, she tried to erase away all the questions from the blackboard of her mind. Somehow, she fell asleep and dreamed of a chain-smoking French detective who was arresting Angie for taking pornographic photos and Jennifer for holding séances in her mother's house. Sam was trying to talk the detective out of placing the two women in jail when Jane Oldsfield appeared in her black dress and took out the time travel disk offering it in lieu of bail money. Then Jane smiled, parting her red lips, and told them all they were never born. Detective Montmart turned into a mewling fat gray cat with a white scar near his whiskers, while Angie morphed into Holly and grew a bushy orange tail. Suddenly, Greg Parsons appeared and took Sam and Jennifer's hands. He grabbed the time travel disk, and the three of them disappeared into the air leaving Jane with the two cats.

CHAPTER NINE

"Very few of us are what we seem."

— AGATHA CHRISTIE

Sam awoke in a cold sweat. When she realized she'd been dreaming, she got up and went to the bathroom where she rinsed her face with cool water. Holly was at her heels expecting breakfast. "Not yet, girl," she told the cat. "I have to get myself together first. Something tells me this is going to be a very difficult day."

The phone rang as she ran water for her shower and removed her stockings in preparation for entering the tub. She couldn't believe she'd actually slept with her nylons on, as well as yesterday's outfit. Running barefoot to the kitchen to answer the phone, she almost stepped on Holly who ducked out of her way. Sam was hesitant as she picked up the receiver and was glad to hear Angie's voice at the other end.

"Why are you so breathless? Have you been up to something without telling me?"

"Angie, you have quite an imagination."

"A dirty mind is a more appropriate term. It can be imaginative, yes, but also downright filthy." She laughed. "So, tell me, Miss Stewart, are you going to Virtual Software this afternoon?"

Sam didn't know how much to tell Angie. "Yes. I was just getting ready."

"Great. I know I promised not to tag along this time, but I'm off for the day so ..."

"No, thanks." The last thing Sam needed was to have Angie tailing her along with Detective Montmart.

"Okay. I wish you lots of luck. Call me when you get back. Are you visiting your mom and sister again?"

"I will if I have time." Sam had no intention of visiting her family when she'd probably be reporting back to Montmart. She was beginning to know what a spy felt like.

"Say hello if you do." Angie paused as if thinking. "Sam, are you okay?"

"Fine. Why?"

"You sound sort of nervous. Did anything happen last night that I should know?"

"Nothing that you should know," Sam answered truthfully. "Thanks for calling. I'll get back to you later."

"Give Greg Parsons my regards."

"I'm sure he'll remember you."

"I am unforgettable. Bye, Sam."

"Bye." Sam hung up the phone and was thankful to get back to her shower. She needed the warmth of the water to relax her, if only momentarily.

After showering, dressing, feeding the cat, and skimming through the newspaper which no longer contained the Virtual Software ad, Sam locked her apartment and headed downstairs. Mr. Clancy didn't interrupt her. He was usually a late riser. As she passed his apartment door, she made a mental note to herself about the spaghetti dinner she'd promised him that night. It wouldn't exactly be a celebration dinner, though, because she had a feeling she'd no longer have nor want this position after her meeting with Virtual Software's acting president this afternoon.

Sam repeated the same journey to Long Island as she had the previous day with Angie, walking to the train bound for Mineola. But, instead of taking a taxi to the Virtual Software Building, she asked the driver to drop her off at the Turnpike Diner a block before the building. It was sunny and brisk out without a hint of showers in the sky or on the wind. Autumn seemed to be arriving early this year with the temperature dipping into the low sixties. She wore a long-sleeved, navy and white dress with a paisley pattern. It was casual yet businesslike and, more importantly, comfortable. *A good outfit for undercover work*, she thought, trying to psyche herself into the spy frame of mind. She wasn't looking forward to this assignment — at least not the spying part. She had to admit that she was looking forward to a second meeting with Greg Parsons, even if Angie would accuse her of having a dirty mind and Detective Montmart suspected Parsons of playing a part in Jane Oldsfield's scheme. Sam couldn't help but be intrigued by a handsome, well-educated man. Perhaps, her dream the previous night featuring Greg as her and her sister's hero was her subconscious' way of telling her that she wanted to trust him. She ordered herself to cease this train of thought as the cab pulled up in front of the diner. *Your subconscious fooled you before with Peter; it can do the same thing with someone new.* Besides, she had more important things to worry about as she contemplated her meeting with Detective Montmart.

She paid the taxi driver and gave him a generous tip before entering the diner. It wasn't quite twelve o'clock, so she wasn't sure if the detective would be there yet. When a blonde, middle-aged woman in a lavender pantsuit asked if she preferred to be seated in the smoking or non-smoking section, she felt strange saying "smoking," because she'd never developed that nasty habit and tried to avoid secondhand smoke. "Actually, I'm meeting someone in the smoking section," she told the hostess, although she didn't know why she was explaining herself.

The woman didn't reply but led her down the left aisle of cream-colored booths with identical cassette player jukeboxes.

In the last booth facing her, a man called out her name as she approached. She didn't know how the detective recognized her because she hadn't given him a description, although Harry or Rod may have. She only knew that she would never have recognized him. There was no resemblance at all to Officer Harry or John Clancy, and the detective was much younger than she'd expected from the sound of his voice. Although he had gray hair, it seemed to be premature because the man looked to be in his late thirties or just the other side of forty.

"Well, I see your companion is already here," the hostess said. "A waitress will be over shortly to take your orders." With that, she walked briskly back to the front of the diner to greet other incoming guests.

Sam approached the detective hesitantly. He'd taken the cigarette he was smoking out of his mouth when he'd called to her and was tapping it against the shell-shaped ashtray in front of him.

"Detective Montmart?" she asked, even though she knew it was him. He was wearing street clothes — a pair of jeans and a blue, v-neck sweater that revealed a small thatch of gray chest hair curlier than that on his head. His eyes were almost the exact same shade as the sweater, a light sky blue. Under the left one, a small white scar was barely noticeable. *The potato head was a gourmet spud in cheap aluminum foil wrapping,* she thought. He reminded her somewhat of a cross between a dignified Hercule Poirot, the French detective created by Agatha Christie, and Columbo, the zany but cute television P.I. portrayed by Peter Falk. He didn't look rich. The sweater could've come off the rack of a "softer side of Sears" display, and she expected that the jeans bore no designer label. She could hardly believe this was the villain of her dream.

"That's me," the gruff telephone voice replied. "Have a seat, Miss Stewart." He picked up his cigarette and waved a wisp of smoke like miniature skywriting toward the opposite bench.

Sam shuffled onto the vinyl cushion. She noticed either the detective or one of the previous diners had chosen a selection from the jukebox. It was the Carly Simon song, "Anticipation," a real oldie and one that ironically summed up her feelings at the moment. Yet no music played. The rusted machine was probably broken.

"Are you ready?" the detective asked, and she was startled at the question until she realized he was referring to the meeting with Greg Parsons.

"Not really. I don't know what this is all about."

"That makes two of us." He took a puff of his cigarette but politely blew it in the other direction. "Miss Oldsfield is a mysterious woman. When I was called in on her case, I found it highly unusual. Her house is like something out of a North Shore Mansion's ad, but she supposedly lives there alone. She came from California originally, but I can't locate any relatives. She could be using an alias. In any case, I think you could be a great help in pinning her down. She and Parsons must be up to something, and it can't be good."

"I don't like to play spy," Sam said. "I'm a lousy liar. My friend, on the other hand, may have done the job justice for you."

"Angie Palmer?"

Sam became angry. "How much checking up on me have you done?"

"I'm a detective, Miss Stewart. My job is to investigate. In fact, you and I have a lot in common. You used to be a librarian, I understand. Did you know that librarians are in the same job category as detectives according to vocational designations? Personality wise, we're both stubborn people because we search until we find answers."

"The difference is that librarians don't usually risk their lives in the search," Sam explained. "And I don't intend to risk mine for your investigation."

Montmart smiled, and Sam was amazed his teeth were so white for someone who smoked heavily. She assumed he had lots of caps or used special whitening toothpaste to fight tobacco stains.

"I'm not sending you to the tigers alone. I'll be right outside the building. In addition, I have something to give you." He reached into his left jeans pocket and took out a small device Sam first feared might be another time-travel disk before she realized it was a bug. She was receiving her official spy apparatus.

"Keep this on you or in your purse, and I'll be able to hear everything that goes on in Parsons' office," the detective told her, handing her the pea-shaped device.

Sam took it cautiously.

"It's not a bomb."

Now it was her turn to smile. "I know what it is, Detective Montmart, and I don't feel any safer. What do you think Parsons and Oldsfield are up to, anyway?"

"Not time travel, that's for sure." He didn't speculate any further because their waitress, a girl who looked sixteen, appeared at their table. Her hair was the same shade as Sam's but worn back in a ponytail. She wore a short black skirt and a low-cut white blouse. Sam viewed her as a kid trying to act sexy, but Montmart seemed to find her appealing because he looked the young woman up and down before taking the menu she offered.

"Are you the special today?" the detective asked.

The waitress seemed embarrassed but pleased at the same time. "Uh, no, Sir, but we do have luncheon specials on the back of the menu." She plunked Sam's menu down hurriedly and walked back to the kitchen.

"Youngsters. They give me a kick," Montmart remarked when the waitress had gone. He looked back at Sam after glancing at his watch, a Woolworth special, that had a corroded gold band that was worn down to a silvery color. "We should aim at getting out of here by a quarter to one so I can get a good spot near the building." Then he added, "I don't mean to rush you or anything. I'm a stickler for punctuality. I think it's a common trait among detectives."

"That's okay. I don't have much of an appetite," Sam replied putting down her menu. "I think I'll just have a salad."

When the waitress returned, Sam noticed her skirt was pulled down an inch or so and her blouse buttoned one notch higher. She took their orders in a businesslike manner avoiding the detective's lusty glare and didn't linger after jotting down their requests.

"It looks like I scared her," Montmart said. "I wouldn't be surprised if she changes that outfit completely before bringing our food."

Sam wasn't amused. "Look, Detective Montmart, I didn't come here to watch you play games with the waitress. In fact, I don't know why I'm here at all. I wish I hadn't gotten involved in the first place, and I may not even have the nerve to go through with this."

The detective's voice and gaze turned serious. "I'm sorry, Miss Stewart. I know I'm asking a lot of you, but I promise I'll make sure there's a minimum of danger involved."

"That doesn't make me feel much safer."

"I realize that, and I'm thankful." The detective reached into the same pocket that had held the bug and dropped a box of Marlboroughs and an old silver lighter on the table. Sam almost laughed when she realized she'd been correct about the brand he smoked, also. Taking another cigarette out of the case, he lit it with the lighter which Sam noticed was engraved with the tarnished initials RM. She wondered what Montmart's first name was – if it was Robert or Russell or even Rod like the young officer. He didn't look like any of those, but most people didn't resemble their first names because everyone had a different idea of what a John, George, Mary, or Jean looked like. Most people got these impressions from early associations such as names of childhood classmates, friends, or relatives or even television or movie stars. Sam knew she didn't look like her idea of a Samantha, the blonde witch Elizabeth Montgomery had portrayed on *Bewitched*.

Sam's thoughts were interrupted by the return of the waitress who brought her salad and Montmart's Diner Special, a thick cheeseburger with fat French fries. The waitress hadn't changed her outfit but scurried away hastily after putting down their plates.

The detective stubbed out his cigarette in the ashtray. "I won't smoke while we eat," he said. "I know that can be annoying."

"Thank you." Sam nibbled on the lettuce and even managed to eat the half tomato that she was surprised to see in the bowl. Mostly, she moved the vegetables to different locations around with her fork.

"That looks like fun," Montmart remarked after biting into a large piece of his burger and swallowing. "Either you're as nervous as you say, or you eat like a bird."

"Guilty of the former. I wish I ate like a bird or like my friend, Angie, who eats less than a bird."

Montmart smiled, and the hazy white scar near his left eye became more pronounced. Sam thought of the pit bulls and couldn't imagine why this man owned such dangerous animals. "You really don't have to worry, Miss Stewart," he said, and Sam didn't know whether he was referring to the effect of the amount she ate on her figure or to the meeting with Greg Parsons or both.

Sam didn't know what made her say, "Detective, do you mind, instead of all this formal Miss and Detective Sir, that we use first names? Mine's Sam; it's really Samantha, but I prefer the shorter version."

"No problem. I was waiting for you to suggest it. I'm Philip, and I don't prefer any other version."

Sam was confused. If his first initial was "P," what or whom did "RM" stand for on his lighter?

As if reading her mind, Philip Montmart put his lighter and the remainder of his cigarette pack back into his jeans pocket. "I don't want to frighten you, further, Sam, but there are some other things about this case I think you should know."

For some reason, the sound of her name on his gravelly voice made Sam feel more comfortable, even though the words that followed should've unnerved her.

"I might as well know all of it," she told him, rummaging around in her greens.

The detective's voice took on that serious note again which was signaled by an even lower raspinness. "When I was called on the Oldsfield case, I investigated Jane Oldsfield's home and found nothing out of the ordinary. It seemed like she just got up one day and left without taking anything with her."

"I read about that in the paper."

"Yes. Well, there's stuff that didn't make the papers. Detectives usually don't like releasing all their info to reporters. I've been doing periodic checks on the house to see if anyone comes or goes. She's been back there. I can bet my license on it."

"I thought you told me you hadn't seen Jane Oldsfield since she disappeared in July."

"I haven't, but I've seen her cat. Or, rather, I've seen a cat hanging around the place. What makes it so unusual is that every time this cat shows up, something disappears from the house – an article of clothing, a book, a piece of jewelry. Most of it is unnoticeable at the time, but I'm very thorough."

"Was it gray?" Sam tossed her fork in her plate and finally abandoned the salad. "The cat you saw. Was he a large gray Tom?"

"How did you know that? Miss Stewart, uh, Sam, is there something you're not telling me?"

"Jane said he belonged to Parsons. She called him Floppy – said he worked for her."

The detective raised a gray eyebrow. "Cats don't work for anyone. They're not like dogs. My pit bulls work for me, and I reward them. Cats expect rewards without working for them. That's what makes them different from dogs."

"Smarter you mean," Sam said, wondering how the topic had digressed to animals.

"Not necessarily, but wiser."

Something in his tone caused Sam to ask, "Do you have cats, also?" even though she couldn't imagine the pit bulls sharing their home with felines.

"My wife did, a pretty Persian named Lulu. She used to share the bed with us." He paused as if unsure whether to continue. Then he added, "that was before the ... before the pit bulls."

"I see." Sam hadn't noticed a ring on the detective's finger, but not all men wore wedding bands. She tried to steer the conversation back on track.

"What do you want me to do today when I meet with Parsons?"

The other gray eyebrow rose, the one above the cheek with the light scar. "Ask questions and listen carefully even though I'll be listening, too. If it gets tough, I'll come and get you. But I don't think Parsons will harm you. He wants something, and we need to find out what that something is. If it's connected with Oldsfield, we'll kill two birds with one stone."

Before Sam could comment, the young waitress returned and asked them if they wanted any dessert. She hoped the detective wasn't going to take advantage of the question and was relieved when he declined the offer by saying they just wanted the check. She wondered what Mrs. Montmart thought of her flirtatious husband. For all Sam knew, the detective might be divorced. He'd referred to his wife's cat in the past tense. Either it had died, or Mrs. Montmart had gotten it in the divorce settlement, while Philip had been left petless until he acquired his dogs.

"We might as well get going," the detective said snapping Sam out of her reverie. He tossed some money on the table and slid out from behind the booth. Sam followed, realizing now as he walked in front of her that he was only about three inches taller than her five-foot two height. That made her even more ill at ease with the thought of him as protector against the tall Greg Parsons.

CHAPTER TEN

"I wish he would explain his explanation."

— BYRON: "DON JUAN. DEDICATION"

Montmart led Sam out of the diner to the parking lot where he opened the passenger door of a fairly new-looking black Toyota. Sam got in, looking for signs of another female's presence, but she knew the Toyota may have been an undercover car and that the family car might be Philip's wife's.

As soon as he was behind the wheel, Montmart lit up again, opening his window with an automatic lever. Taking a few puffs and exhaling out the window, he stubbed the half-finished cigarette out in the car ashtray that was already full of blackened cigarette butts. Sam interpreted this action as one of nervousness, which didn't make her any less anxious.

They drove the short distance in silence with the window still down and cool air billowing inside. The detective didn't say anything until they stopped in front of the glass Virtual Software building. As Sam was sitting there, not sure if she should get out, Montmart turned to her and said in his serious deep voice, "Be careful, Sam."

On unsteady legs, Sam got out and walked into the building's front entrance. She didn't look back at the detective but could feel his cool blue eyes watching her. For encouragement, Sam felt the bug in the pocket of her dress, which would act as an invisible umbilical cord between her and the detective. She only prayed he wouldn't have to come in after her, gun drawn. But now that she thought of it, Montmart didn't seem to carry a gun. The only items in his jean's pockets were the lighter with the mysterious initials and his cigarettes.

When Sam was on the elevator, riding to the second floor, she realized what was missing from the last time she was in this building — the crowds. The hordes of people waiting in line for an interview at the software company were gone. She was alone in the elevator and hadn't passed anyone except a few secretaries in the hall of the lower floor offices when she'd entered the building. *Word must've gotten out that the job was taken,* she thought. Her already queasy stomach lurched as the elevator came to a stop on the Virtual Software floor and opened to a deserted hallway. Sam was glad she hadn't eaten much lunch because she knew she would've lost it before she even got to the room.

When Sam arrived at the door to the Virtual Software office, she noticed it was closed. For a moment, she considered leaving and saying Parsons had forgotten about the appointment. She knew that would be chickening out, and, like the proverbial cat, curiosity was killing her.

She tapped lightly at the door and wasn't surprised that there was no answer. Maybe Parsons really had forgotten. She tried the doorknob and found it loose but hesitated to let herself in even though she could see a light underneath the door, a pale fluorescent footnote beyond the carpet.

Sam wasn't the courageous type, but she found the strength to slide the door open gently without making a sound. Why was she trying to be quiet? If Parsons was here, didn't she want him to know she'd arrived for their appointment?

Feeling more like a spy every minute, Sam slipped into the outer office where she expected to see an angry Mrs. McGee staring at her from the desk. Instead, the secretary's chair was empty. Suddenly, she heard a noise. It was coming from the back room where she and Angie had taken turns interviewing and being interviewed by Greg Parsons the day before. The sound was like that a computer might make when booting up with the rhythmic tapping of keyboard keys following.

Sam struggled to keep herself from calling out. Why was she being deliberately stealthy? She inched forward following the yellow light trail in front of her. As she came in sight of Parsons' office door, she saw the man sitting in his desk chair, dark blond head bent as he typed on his computer.

Sam's conscience got the best of her, and she cleared her throat. "Excuse me, Mr. Parsons. I let myself in because no one answered my knock. Should I wait outside?"

The acting president of Virtual Software had been so intent on his typing that he jumped at the interruption but soon collected himself. "That's all right, Miss Stewart. I'm ready now. Please come in. Sorry no one was here to greet you, but my secretary is off today, and I get absorbed when I work."

Sam entered the room, and Parsons gestured for her to sit in the seat she'd occupied last time. The room seemed larger to her today with bright sunshine flooding through the drawn mini blinds competing with the luminescence of the fluorescent lamps at either end of Parsons' desk. Sam knew her mother would have a heart attack about the waste of money by keeping the lights on in the room in daylight.

Parsons regarded her as he turned away from his monitor. "I'm glad you've come back. I wasn't sure you would."

"I wasn't sure either."

Then he said something that startled her and was more typical of an outspoken "Angie statement" than what she'd expected would come from this reserved businessman. "Has she visited you yet?"

"If you mean Jane Oldsfield, yes. She was at my apartment yesterday."

"You haven't told anyone about her, have you?"

"Just Angie, and she thinks I was dreaming."

"I mean the authorities. You haven't called the police?"

Sam didn't like to lie because she wasn't good at it. "No," she said unable to look into his blue eyes. She was sure he recognized the falsehood of her reply, but he continued without a pause.

"Good. So, I guess you're waiting for an explanation. I can't blame you. If I were in your shoes, I'd be questioning my sanity."

Although Sam tried to remain focused on his words, what little they were revealing, she found herself comparing him with Detective Montmart. Dressed more formally in a gray business suit, his complexion and hair coloring were much lighter while his eyes were deeper but just as unreadable.

"I thought I was going crazy at one point, but now I know I did see what I saw." Sam was wondering how much of this Montmart was hearing and hoped she was coming across as confident as she was trying to sound for the benefit of both men.

Parsons logged off his computer, and she heard the familiar Windows shutdown routine. He was allowing her to have his complete attention, or was he commanding hers?

"Jane and I were involved in a very special project, Miss Stewart. We were trying to create a software program that would allow individuals to travel to places both local and foreign without the aid of commonplace transportation systems such as airplanes, trains, or cars. If we succeeded, the benefits to mankind would have been astronomical. Can you imagine the time and cost savings of such travel? It would've been the answer to traffic jams and jet lag. We were on the brink of bringing this new technology to fruition when Jane discovered the program had some major bugs. I won't bore you with the technical details. Let's just say my partner found that our travel program had the capacity to not only transport individuals to other places but also to other times." Parsons stared at her as if transfixed by his story, regardless of the fact that it sounded rehearsed. She wondered if he'd told this story to anyone else or had memorized it especially for her. She pictured Detective Montmart in his Toyota laughing so hard his scar was cracking.

"That's quite a story. Is that where Jane Oldsfield disappeared to – another time period?"

Parsons must've known she didn't believe a word he said. She gave him credit for continuing the tale. "Jane travels back and forth between many time periods. She's trying to stabilize the program so that the proper coordinates are aligned. You see, presently the time travel feature of the program is defective. When it's activated, one never knows exactly to what year he or she will be transported."

It reminded Sam of a television show she once watched called "Quantum Leap" where a group of time travelers "leaped" between different times but never knew where they would land. Sam continued playing along. Her only concern was that Montmart would come storming in when he'd heard enough. "So, what is my role in all this, or, rather, what will my role be if I choose to accept this position?"

Parsons steepled his fingers together as she'd seen him do on the previous visit when he was considering what to say. "The description of the job in the ad I placed was correct. I need someone who has a background in history and enough knowledge of software to help me stop Jane from what she's attempting. That will involve extensive travel, but not the kind I think you expected."

"You want me to go back in time?" As ridiculous as the proposition sounded, Sam couldn't help but betray the fear in her voice.

"Or forward. The time travel component is capable of transporting someone up to twelve months into the future and anytime into the past." Parsons paused as if to give himself as well as Sam a chance to digest that information. Then he opened the center drawer of his desk and extracted an identical time travel disk to the one Jane Oldsfield had in Sam's apartment.

Sam gasped as she recognized the object. She fought to retain her control. "I still don't believe this, but if what you're saying is true, what am I supposed to do in these time periods?"

Parsons placed the disk in the center of his desk partway between him and Sam. "That will all be covered in the training. I won't expect you to take your first trip for at least a month. Basically, your job will be to find and deactivate or destroy Foundation Markers."

Now Sam felt as if she'd moved from a spy adventure to a science fiction epic. "What are Foundation Markers?" she asked.

"They're another term for the time-travel disks that reflect their function to lock in coordinates into real-time mode. In non-technical jargon that means that, placed in the correct location on the correct date, a dozen Foundation Markers or Time-Travel disks, will enable the stabilization necessary for anyone to travel to any time period in history anywhere in the world. The consequences of creating such a tool would make the atom bomb's inventor uneasy not to mention the ethical ramifications of being able to change time at one's will."

"Let me make sure I follow you," Sam said. "Jane Oldsfield is trying to place twelve Foundation Markers, Time-Travel disks, or whatever else you call them, in different time periods and time zones to act as bookmark type place holders."

Parsons smiled, and she noticed how it lit up his face. He seemed to be a man who liked to laugh and wasn't at ease with the serious role in which he found himself. She wondered if the athletic build and dark tan were the results of traveling to tropical climes or Egyptian times but reminded herself that she shouldn't make the mistake of taking the story too literally.

"That's a very good analogy," he said. "The Foundation Markers act as bookmarks that hold both place and time settings. And, if you notice," he picked up the time-travel disk again and turned it around slowly on his palm, "the disks, themselves, are very much like compasses. Jane did most of the designing. She really is brilliant. It's a shame she became so greedy." His voice took on a regretful tone, and Sam was suddenly reminded of the way he'd spoken about the cat he once had.

"Did you have a gray cat named Floppy?" she asked impulsively.

Parsons nearly dropped the Time-Travel Disk. "Have you seen him? Is he okay?"

Sam could've laughed at his concern, but she knew she'd be just as concerned if Holly were missing. "He seems fine to me. He's a bit overweight; but, otherwise, he looks great."

The relief on the man's face was touching. She knew he couldn't be acting this part.

"What did Jane mean when she said the cat was working for her?"

"It's a long story; but when Jane argued with me about the proper use of the Time-Travel Disks, she implanted a microchip in Floppy that would allow him to travel back and forth through time and act as her 'Grounder.'"

"Is that what she meant by saying that she switched with him and why I saw the cat right before she appeared in my apartment?"

"Yes. Floppy is her grounder to the present time. She has the eleven Foundation Markers; the twelfth is in the circuits implanted in the cat."

"Excuse me if I seem a little naïve about your technical terms, but what is a 'grounder' and how does it work?" Sam hoped she was asking the right questions and not exacerbating the listening detective who was probably getting impatient with all the small talk.

87

"I know you're eager to learn everything, and I don't blame you. But I'd rather not confuse you further. The next time we meet, I'll show you the prototypes and Jane's journal. For some reason, she didn't take it with her. That's what enabled me to duplicate the disks."

"Now, wait a minute, Mr. Parsons." It was Sam's turn to be impatient. "You can't give me half an explanation and see me off. If I'm going to be involved in this, I want the whole scoop. Besides, I don't appreciate midnight or any other time of day visits from your partner."

"She's not my partner," Parsons corrected her. "She used to be but not after she convoluted our project and used my cat as a guinea pig." His voice was rising in anger, but he lowered it when he saw Sam's reaction. "I'm sorry, Miss Stewart. You're an innocent bystander in all this, and, yes, you deserve a complete explanation."

Here it comes, Sam thought, *turn on your tape recorder if you have one, Detective Montmart.*

Instead of continuing, he stood up behind his desk. Sam felt a bit overwhelmed and just a touch frightened at the tall man's expression as he looked down at her. "It would take me much too long to explain everything, so I'm going to give you some reading material for this evening. When you return tomorrow, you can ask whatever questions you feel haven't been adequately answered in the journal."

Sam now felt like a student being given a homework assignment. "What makes you so sure I'll be back tomorrow, Mr. Parsons?"

The expression the man made was even more disturbing than his earlier countenance. His eyes were stormy. "I didn't choose you by accident, Miss Stewart. I've been to the future, and I know you'll return."

Sam got up from her seat to face him on a more even level, despite the fact that he still towered above her. "This is a little too much for me," she said, "Foundation Markers and Grounders, cats and greedy women, and now you say I'm destined to do your bidding. What do I get in return for all this? A six-figure income hardly seems worth it."

Suddenly, the darkness was gone from his face as if the sun behind the clouds had reemerged. His smile was dazzling. "Is saving the world compensation enough for you, Samantha? But, don't worry, you'll be paid the advertised salary in phase 2 of the project when I deactivate the time-travel mode and redesign the disks for their original purpose — travel between states and countries."

The use of her first name by him should've warned her. If this man really was as demented as his words seemed to justify, why was she still asking questions and listening to his answers? She should be making her getaway, running back to the detective, and never coming back.

Parsons opened a desk drawer again – this time one of the larger ones on his left side. Sam half expected him to take out a gun and shoot her dead. Crazy people were their most dangerous when they were friendly. Had she read that in some psychology book at the MBL? She couldn't remember. She only knew that she held her breath as he retrieved a thick, spiral-bound notebook and placed it on his desk within her reach.

"This is Jane's journal. It's a complete record of our project. Jane was meticulous about organization."

Sam could imagine the delight of the detective when she brought this goody back to him. She wondered if Parsons and Oldsfield could be locked away in an insane asylum by this evidence alone.

"I don't understand," she said, wondering again why she was taking the time to question him, "If this journal is so impor-tant, why are you letting me have it? And, what if Jane returns to my apartment and takes it?"

"Don't worry. She knows exactly where it is. If she hasn't

taken it yet, she never will." He sighed, and the clouds seemed to cover the sun as they passed across his face. "I know you don't believe any of this now but try to keep an open mind. In the twentieth century, as in every previous century, great advances were made which never seemed possible to those who lived at earlier times. Until relatively recently, no one would have conceived of a worldwide network of computers such as the Internet. Time travel isn't a foreign concept. People have toyed with the idea for ages."

"Yes, they have," Sam admitted, "from H.G. Wells to science fiction writers, but the operative word is 'fiction.' Time is not a continuum. When it's over, it's gone." Why was she still arguing with this man? The detective would probably be coming in after her in a few minutes.

"That's where you're wrong, Miss Stewart, but you'll realize that very shortly." He slid the book forward, and she took it. The meeting was adjourned.

"I'll see you again at one tomorrow. If Jane contacts you, call me." He tore a sheet of notepaper from a pad on his desk, scribbled a phone number on it, and passed it to her. "If I'm not at the office number, call me at home. Any time."

Sam nodded. She was all out of words. She was beginning to get a headache and was relieved that she could finally get out into the fresh air. She needed to breathe and clear her head. Unfortunately, she knew the detective was waiting for her. She really would've preferred to have a few minutes alone right now to contemplate her next move. She took the paper with Parsons' home number on it and started for the door.

"One more thing, Miss Stewart."

She turned back, wondering why he had returned to using her surname. "Yes?"

"Thank you." The way he said it made her feel guilty about the bug in her pocket, but did he already know about that? For a second, Sam wanted to believe the time-travel story was true and that Greg Parsons had indeed gone forward in time and chosen her because the future had told him she was the one who could help. But she knew in her heart that the reality outside Virtual Software's door consisted of a place where time travel didn't exist and people who believed in such things were crazy. Why did she wish Parsons wasn't? Why did she want him to be right?

CHAPTER ELEVEN

"The destiny of mankind is not decided by material computation. When great causes are on the move in the world ... we learn that we are spirits, not animals, and that something is going on in space and time, and beyond space and time, which, whether we like it or not, spells duty."

— CHURCHILL'S RADIO BROADCAST TO AMERICA
ON RECEIVING THE HONORARY DEGREE OF
DOCTOR OF LAWS FROM THE UNIVERSITY OF
ROCHESTER, NEW YORK [JUNE 16, 1941]

Detective Philip Montmart waited for her in his black Toyota in Virtual Software's parking lot. She surprised him when she came up to the car, gripping the notebook in her hands. He surprised her even more by being slumped back with the driver's seat in a prone position. For a second, she feared someone had bumped him off. Then she realized he was only sleeping but sleeping at full attention, like a panther in the jungle awake for primeval guard duty. The radio was playing a country tune that sounded like a Loretta Lynn song. If she wasn't so high strung after her episode with Parsons, she probably would've laughed at the sight.

Montmart sprang up straight, pushing his seat into an upright position. "Sam," he said. "That was quick."

She couldn't believe it. All the time she thought he'd been listening to her in case she ran into trouble, he was listening to cowboy ballads!

She opened the door to the car and got in angrily. "Why did you give me a bug if you weren't monitoring me?" She couldn't help but also notice a half-dozen cigarette butts in the ashtray. The cad had been smoking on the job, too.

"I knew you'd be okay," he said. "You're tough. I notice you brought me back some evidence."

Sam hugged the Oldsfield journal to her chest. "I don't think I'll give it to you now."

Montmart inserted his key into the ignition and started the car. Instead of commenting, he pretended he hadn't heard her. She suddenly felt empathetic toward his wife.

"We'd better get out of here before Parsons realizes you weren't alone. We can go back to the diner if you'd like or maybe you'd prefer a park since it's a nice day."

Sam hadn't been thinking about the weather, but now that he mentioned it, she noticed the sunshine. A balmy breeze sailed through the open window. "A park would be nice," she replied coldly, "if you don't mind driving me back to the city. We could talk in Washington Square which isn't too far from my apartment."

"That sounds fair enough to me. But while we're out here, would you like to stop and visit your sister and mother first?"

Not another one who was intent on seeing her fulfill her familial duty, and she was right about his having investigated her background. She wondered if he also knew she had a scar on her left hip from a bicycle fall she had at twelve.

"Aren't you eager to hear what happened at my meeting?" she asked as they drove down Hempstead Turnpike past the

Turnpike Diner where a young waitress had learned her lesson about flirting so openly.

"I can wait. I'm very patient. About the book, though, I'll have to confiscate it. I'll make you a copy."

"Okay. I guess there won't be any harm in my visiting Mom and Jennifer, although I'd like to keep it short. I'm tired, and I have a headache."

Sam was glad that he got the hint and turn off the radio. The wailing was grating on what was left of her nerves. She celebrated too quickly. He'd simply substituted one annoying habit for another, as he reached in his jeans pocket for a cigarette. "You can tell your relatives I'm an old friend from Queens College that you'd gotten together with for lunch," he added lighting the Marlborough.

He knew everything about her, and he didn't have to travel through time to get the information. "My mother is very good at detecting when I lie."

"Most mothers are." Laugh lines formed around Montmart's eyes, emphasizing his scar in the windshield's sunlight. "Don't worry. I'll make the explanations. I'm good at white lies."

Sam felt sorrier for his wife every minute. "That makes me more comfortable," she said sarcastically.

"I never lie unless it's necessary, and I make sure the lie doesn't hurt anyone."

Sam didn't know what made her say it, but (as they turned onto the Long Island Expressway which eventually became Grand Central Parkway and would take them into the city via a choice of bridges), she replied, "Is that why your wife left you?" She regretted the words as soon as they were out of her mouth, and regretted them even more when the detective said, a pitch lower in his gravelly voice, "RoseAnn left because she died." He stubbed out his cigarette and ground it into the car's ashtray. Those were the last words either of them said until they arrived at Sam's mother's house. Sam felt so bad about her faux pas that she didn't even put in a snide remark about how the detective knew the exact address and how to get there without her assistance.

When Montmart pulled up in front of the house, Sam noticed her mother's car was missing, but Jennifer's Camaro was in the driveway. The front door opened as soon as they started up the walk, Montmart behind Sam. Both were retaining their silence after Sam had awkwardly caused the detective's revelation that he wasn't divorced but was a widower.

Jennifer stood at the door in a white sleeveless T-shirt and denim shorts. She was still dressed for summer, although fall was less than two weeks away. Sam remembered those days when sacrificing warmth to show some leg was preferable to covering up the view eligible college men wanted to see. Her sister wasn't using the bait for a ring because most men her age weren't snapping up that line yet. Now that Sam was an ancient thirty-two, she dressed more conservatively hoping that she would attract a more marriage-minded audience.

Jennifer held open the door. "Hey, Sis, what are you doing here again in the same week? You came at the right time. I was just finished polishing my nails. If they weren't dry, I wouldn't have been able to open the door for you."

"What a pleasant greeting," Sam said, stepping into the house. "And I see you're using a shade for Halloween, even though you're dressed for Fourth of July."

Jennifer looked down at her black nails. "Black is in at college now, but I forgot you wouldn't know that."

Montmart, who'd stepped into the house behind Sam, cleared his throat and then exclaimed, "Excuse me for interrupting you ladies from such an important topic, but I'd like to introduce myself. I'm a friend of Sam's from Queen's College, Philip Montmart. Sam and I had lunch on the Island, and I convinced her to stop and visit her family."

Jennifer tossed back her blonde braids, which Sam thought made her look younger and less sexy than she wanted to appear. "So that's why she's here. Welcome to Sam's dysfunctional habitat, Phil. I'm her freeloading sister, Jennifer, and her hypochondriac mom is, where else, at the doctors."

Montmart bent down and petted one of the cats that came over to circle his legs. A few others were waiting behind the friendlier animal to see if the stranger was safe and if he had any food for them.

"Those are my mom's cats," Jennifer continued when she saw his reaction to the white one. "That's Snowball. I named him. I name most of them. Mom takes every one that comes to the door, and, occasionally, they multiply. Then we fix them. Do you have cats, Phil?"

Sam was afraid the question would set Montmart off again as a reminder of his wife, but the detective seemed to have gotten over his somberness. "Not now. Currently, I have pit bulls."

"Wow!" Jennifer sounded impressed. "One of my boyfriends had a pit bull. It maimed his neighbor. They're suing. The dog had to be put down."

"My dogs are trained. They won't harm a fly without my permission." His words seemed to imply that the pit bulls would kill on command.

Jennifer's interest in her sister's guest seemed to dwindle, as her interest in most things usually didn't last longer than five minutes. When they were kids, Sam used to tease her younger sister by saying she had the attention span of a flea. As an adult, she knew that analogy had proved to be pretty close to the mark.

"You two can hang out if you want, but there's not much food in the fridge," Jennifer told them. "I'll be in my room if you need me. I have to do my toenails now." With that, she cantered away. Sam couldn't help but notice an extra sway to her hips as if she would've flirted with Montmart if she didn't believe he was her sister's boyfriend and maybe even in spite of it.

"Well, I've done my duty," Sam said. "Are you ready to take me back to the city now?"

Before the detective could answer, there was a scream from down the hall. Montmart, his detective's training showing, was off in a flash bounding toward Sam's sister's bedroom, nearly knocking several cats out of the way. Sam followed at a slower pace, figuring her sister's scream was for spilt nail polish or some other insignificant disaster.

When Sam arrived in the room behind the detective, she saw her sister clutching what looked like a stuffed animal. Sam hadn't been in her sister's room in years, although they'd once shared a bedroom on the other side of the house. This room had been a den that her mother converted into a room for Jennifer when she turned eight. The fifteen-year-old Sam kept the old room but wasn't permitted to change it in any way. Jennifer, on the other hand, got a completely new bedroom set. The old feeling of jealousy returned as Sam surveyed the adult bedroom of her sister that hadn't changed much from her pre-teen years. A frilly pink canopy stood over the queen-sized bed that accommodated red, heart-shaped pillows and a half-dozen teddy bears. The wallpaper featured a teddy-bear pattern, too, and must've come from a juvenile pattern book. A white vanity sat near the window. Before the oval-shaped mirror lay an assortment of expensive cosmetics. The doors of the walk-in closet her father had built for his youngest daughter stood open on the opposite side of the room revealing some of its lavish contents, designer jeans and short shorts along with a variety of tank and tube tops and a collection of shoes that would rival Imelda Marcos' collection. In the corner, next to the bed where Jennifer stood, was the focal point of the room — a large mahogany bookcase with four levels that contained not books but fifty or more beanbag animals with heart-shaped tags. Jennifer embraced one of these animals against her chest. Sam now saw that it wasn't an animal but a white ghost that would fit into a nice Halloween display the following month.

"Oh, Spooky," Jennifer muttered as she held the stuffed toy to her. Then, when she realized she had an audience, she looked up. "Sorry if I frightened you guys, but there was a beast in here when I came in that almost damaged one of my Beanie Babies.

Spooky is worth a lot to me, not only because he's retired and a collectible, but also because it took me so long to locate him. I had to go all the way to a Hallmark store in New Jersey, would you believe?"

Montmart zeroed in on the first half of her statement, ignoring the latter, which he'd probably negated as "bullshit." "What beast was in your room?"

"A cat. Not one of my mother's. A big fat gray cat. He was on my Beanie shelf and knocked Spooky to the floor. He would've ripped him apart and tore out his beans if I hadn't screamed and frightened him away."

The detective's scar was creasing, a sure sign he was holding back laughter. Sam didn't find the situation as funny because she recognized the description of Parsons' cat, Floppy – indicating that Jane Oldsfield would shortly join them. Or was she being paranoid? Any fat gray cat could've run in the house when Jennifer opened the door to let them in. Sam didn't want to wait around to see.

"Well, since your ghost beanbag is safe and sound, I guess the feline terrorist didn't succeed in the assassination," she told her sister and then nodded toward Montmart. "That means we can leave."

"Stop laughing at me." Jennifer spat out the words, even though Sam wasn't the one who was laughing.

Montmart, a true detective, took this opportunity before a sisterly battle ensued to ask questions. "Excuse me, Jennifer, but it seems a bit silly to me. With all the cats your mother has, don't any of them touch your toys?"

"They're not toys; they're collectibles. And, no, I've trained all the cats to leave my belongings alone. When that gray animal appeared, I was furious."

Sam winced at her sister's terminology. "Appeared" was the operative word. Because she didn't want to witness any other appearances, especially those by a woman who favored the color black but wasn't in mourning, Sam backed out of the room, hoping the detective would follow. Unfortunately, he wasn't done interrogating the witness.

"This fat cat you saw, where did it go after it left your room?"

"How should I know? You two stormed in here. Didn't you see where it went?" Jennifer returned Spooky to his place of honor between a lion and a kangaroo.

"I saw lots of cats in the hall," Montmart explained, "but none of them were fat gray ones. Is it possible the animal is still in this room somewhere?"

Jennifer shrugged. "I doubt it, but he couldn't have just disappeared."

Sam winced again. That was precisely what must've happened which meant that Oldsfield was on her way.

Before Sam had a chance to convince Montmart to abandon his investigation and take her back to the city where, ironically, she felt safer alone in her apartment than here in this house in the suburbs with her sister and her stuffed animals, a familiar voice said, "If you're looking for Floppy, he's back in colonial Philadelphia watching Betsy sew the flag. She really did sew the first one, you know."

"What the?" Montmart's half-startled exclamation served as introduction to the woman in the long black dress.

"Hello again, Sam. I didn't really want to visit you here, but Greg gave you my book. He wasn't supposed to do that."

"Who are you?" The detective asked. Before Jane could answer, he recognized her from her photos. "My God, you're Jane Oldsfield."

"That's me." She walked into Jennifer's room and sat on the edge of the canopy bed. "And I know all of you, even if one of you doesn't know me yet."

Jennifer took exception to the woman making herself at home in her domain. "Whoever you are, lady, this is my room and that's my bed. Get off it."

Sam had a sudden feeling of deja vu before she realized that this scene was very similar to one she'd dreamed recently. The only person missing from it was Greg Parsons.

Jane pretended not to hear Jennifer. "As I was saying, Sam, my ex-partner left you some material. I know it's still in Philip's car, and I really don't mind both of you reading it. It's just that it can't be turned over to the authorities or anyone outside our little circle. Do you understand?"

Jennifer looked as if she was going to scream again. "Is this a friend of yours, too Sam? She has the manners of a bug."

Under less trying circumstances, Sam would've laughed at that remark as a comeback to her favorite insect comparison for her sister's less than ideal traits. "She's no friend of mine, Jennifer. Call the police if she doesn't leave."

"Now, Sam, don't be so harsh." Jane reclined against one of the heart-shaped pillows. "I'll be on my way after you promise me what I asked. I have to get back to Betsy. She promised to fix one of the buttons on my skirt." She indicated a loose button near the hem of her black dress. "And don't worry about Greg's cat. I won't send him back here. I'll divert the setting back to my house. The switch doesn't have to be to the same place, you see, just the same time." She turned toward Montmart who was studying her from under hooded gray eyebrows. "You have to promise about my journal, too, detective. The last thing I need is for the FBI to get their hands on it."

"Detective?" Jennifer said the word like a curse. "Is that what this is? He's not an old school chum; he's a private eye you hired to check me out? Did Mom put you up to this, Sam? No, she wouldn't. She trusts me. You've always been jealous of me. You'd love to see me in jail, but I'm clean, Sis. I'm not doing drugs or anything else. Maybe I should be, though, with a sister like you."

Before Sam could deny the accusations, Montmart said, "Don't blame Sam. I was the one who asked her to concoct the story about our being friends. I thought it would be easier. I'm a detective, but I'm not here to investigate you. I'm here to investigate Miss Oldsfield, and I see she's finally turned up." He faced the woman on the bed. "I'll make sure no one shows your book to anybody yet, but I'd like to know what you've been up to for the past several months and what exactly you want with Miss Stewart."

Jane smiled that arrogant smile Sam detested. "After reading that notebook, you'll know precisely what I've been up to the past several months and what I want with Samantha. Actually, what I want with all of you." She darted her dark eyes from one to the other as she scanned the room like a sly fox seeking its prey. "Greg will try to convince you to join his team. He'll spout ethics and morality until it makes you gag. The only thing I spout is good old monetary gain. I've always had money, but I could use more. The rest of you don't seem too well off to me. You'd be fools to give up your chances for fame and fortune."

"You still haven't answered my question," Montmart persisted. "You can be sure I'll read every word of your notes, but could you summarize this grand plan you want us to participate in?"

Oldsfield considered the request. But, instead of answering, she took the now familiar object she referred to as the Time-Travel Disk from one of her skirt pockets and held it out to the detective just a few inches beyond his grasp like bait she wasn't intending to offer easily. "What you're all about to witness is my departure to another time and place. Sam and Philip will have an opportunity to travel with me one day soon. Greg Parsons will give you the means but for his own purpose. For those who follow the path I've outlined in the journal, there will be great rewards. For those who follow Greg's path, there will be nothing beyond today." She tapped some keys on the TTD with her long red nails and winked her left eye at the transfixed group. Before her black lashes were fully raised, she was gone. Jennifer's bed was empty except for the heart pillows.

"Where did she go?" Jennifer asked in a trembling voice.

"Back to Colonial Philadelphia," Sam replied. "I thought I was crazy at first, but now you've all seen her disappearing act."

Montmart stared at the bed. "Don't touch anything. She's got to be here somewhere." He closed the bedroom door behind him and began canvassing the room. He checked under the bed and in the closet, banging walls to see if any of them had a secret passage.

"That won't help," Sam told him. "I would never have admitted this until now, but I think she's telling the truth — that they're both telling the truth. Parsons and Oldsfield have created a way to time travel, and they need us to help them in their opposite causes. Jane wants to perfect the method and sell it to the highest bidder; Greg wants to deactivate it and/or destroy it because it'll allow people to change time at their own will."

The detective didn't seem to be listening. He was still scouring the room for traces of the missing woman. Jennifer, on the other hand, was listening intently. "Are you sure that's it, Sam, or could it be a psychic phenomenon? At school, we're learning about out-of-body experiences."

"Yes, but we saw her body, and it's gone."

Montmart paused in his detection of the connecting bathroom and stepped back into the bedroom. "I still think there has to be a reasonable explanation for all this, and now I'm more eager than ever to read that notebook."

"What notebook?" Jennifer asked.

Sam knew her sister wouldn't be of any help to them, but Jennifer was already involved, as were she and the detective.

"Greg Parsons, Jane Oldsfield's partner, gave me her journal to read before meeting with him again tomorrow. That's what I was doing on the Island this afternoon and why Detective Montmart is with me. Parsons and Oldsfield worked together at Virtual Software, a travel software company that was advertising for help in their research department. I answered the ad, and the rest is history, or will be history, as the case may be." Sam summarized for Jennifer.

"Cool!" Jennifer's response was enthusiastic. "Why don't you get the book now, and we can read it together? Maybe I can do my mid-term project on this."

"Wait a minute," Montmart cautioned. "This is highly confidential information. I'm in charge here, and I'll read the book first. This isn't a game. It may be a crime. There's no such thing as time travel, so Miss Oldsfield is covering up something else. I don't know how she got out of here so fast, but I know she didn't go to another time because the past is a place where none of us can ever travel once it's passed us by."

Sam wondered why Philip said the words with such vehemence.

"It would be great, wouldn't it, to go back in time," Jennifer exclaimed ignoring the hot blue flames in the detective's eyes.

"That could be extremely dangerous," Sam said. "And I hope we don't ever find out."

"Don't worry, we won't." Montmart, having given up his search, opened the bedroom door. "Are you ready to go back to New York, Sam?"

"What if she returns?" Sam knew who Jennifer was referring to.

"I don't think she will. She seems to want this meeting with you and Parsons to take place tomorrow. In the meantime, we have a lot of reading to do."

"I thought you said you were reading the book first?"

The blue flames were slowly burning down like a tired candle. "I think we should share our findings."

"What about me?" Jennifer asked like a child excluded from an adult discussion. "Oldsfield said I was going to be in on it, too."

Before Sam could reply, Philip shook his head. "Not yet, Jennifer. It isn't safe to have too many people involved at once. Sam was involved from the start, and I'm the professional here. We'll fill you in as soon as we know anything for sure."

Jennifer made a face that was half-pouting, half-defiant. "Is that a promise?"

"Yes, and don't say anything to anyone, especially your mother."

Sam almost laughed at the thought of Jennifer telling their mother and the consequences that might bring. She'd be in the hospital if she heard about this.

"Mom would have a coronary," she said as if reading Sam's mind. "I couldn't be that cruel."

"Shall we, Sam?" Montmart asked in his gravelly voice which sounded lighter.

Sam looked at her sister. "Will you be okay, Jennifer?"

"Of course. Mom will be back soon. Not that she'd be much protection, but she wouldn't hesitate to call 911."

Neither Sam nor Montmart found that amusing. "Just be careful," the detective told her as he walked out into the hall. Sam followed with a cautioning look at Jennifer.

As they left the house, Sam asked, "Are you sure she'll be safe? As much as I dislike my sister, I don't want to see her come to any harm."

"She'll be fine. You're the one who has to worry."

They were standing outside the passenger door of the Toyota. "That sure makes me feel better," Sam mocked the detective.

He took his keys out of his jeans pocket and unlocked the car door. "I'm not taking you back to the city yet," he said. "At least, we'll be making two stops before that."

Sam didn't have the opportunity to ask which side trips they'd be making because Montmart was already in the driver's seat. She noticed his manners didn't extend to opening her door.

It was still a nice day out, although a light wind was kicking up. As Sam sat against the black Naugahyde seat with the notebook back on her lap, she rolled her window down to dispel some of the smoky air that had been trapped inside the car while they were in the house. She wondered why Montmart hadn't smoked in the house but figured it was another way of his being polite without being overly nice. Her assumption was confirmed when the detective took out his lighter and a cigarette. As he started the car's engine, he lit the cigarette.

"You know those things cause cancer," she said buckling up her seat belt.

"Everything causes something," Montmart replied. "And if you don't succumb to any disease, you get killed in an accident. Life's for us to enjoy."

"Is that your motto?"

The detective backed out of the driveway, trying to avoid Jennifer's sports car. His eyes were on the road and not Sam as he said, "Has been since my wife died."

Sam wanted to pursue this topic, if only for her own curiosity. She asked the obvious follow-up question. "Did your wife die in an accident?"

Montmart's hands tightened on the steering wheel. They'd cleared the driveway and were headed down the road in the opposite direction from where they'd come. "She was murdered."

Sam almost choked on her own saliva. "Oh, my God. I'm sorry."

The detective changed the subject as he exhaled a puff of smoke from his cigarette. "We'll be visiting Oldsfield's house to check if the cat is around. I want you to see the place, anyway. Then it's off to my house. You can meet Rover and his family, have a bite to eat, and help me digest the information in that book."

This wasn't the way Sam had planned to spend the rest of her day, visiting cats and dogs. She'd promised Mr. Clancy a spaghetti dinner, and she knew Holly needed to be fed, too.

"Look, I'd really love to help, but I have plans for this evening. I have to get home."

"You'll have to cancel those plans." Montmart's voice was as sharp as the turn he took around the corner.

"What if I can't?"

Montmart pulled over to the side of the road. "Then get out now and leave the notebook."

Sam almost wanted to take him up on the challenge. She could walk back to her mother's house, call a cab to the train station, and get the hell back to her apartment. On the other hand, she was too involved and curious now not to see this through.

Philip was looking at her, and the temperature was dropping in those icy blue eyes. *What was he so angry about?*

"Let's go," Sam relented.

CHAPTER TWELVE

"In completing one discovery we never fail to get an imperfect knowledge of others of which we could have no idea before, so that we cannot solve one doubt without creating several new ones."

— PRIESTLEY "EXPERIMENTS AND
OBSERVATIONS ON DIFFERENT KINDS OF AIR"
[1775-1786]

Old Brookville could be considered the Palm Beach of Long Island. It's a community of well-established, wealthy, primarily senior citizens who live in homes with names on their own private streets. The Gold Coast, North Shore, elites who spend the winters in warmer climes and the summers teeing off at nearby country club golf courses. This is the setting, Sam discovered, where both Jane Oldsfield and Philip Montmart resided. She was surprised to learn Montmart was practically Jane's neighbor, if only by a few hundred acres. She was even more surprised to discover her earlier assumption about the detective had been correct in that he was rich. He hadn't dressed nor acted the part. And if he had so much money, why was he working in a blue-collar job? These and other questions would have to wait for answers because Montmart was pulling up into Split Branch Road where a large white house could be seen beyond the long, tree-shaded driveway.

"Miss Oldsfield's home," Philip announced. "The security system is still on, although I can bypass it if you'd like to get a look inside. The cat usually hangs around on the sunporch."

Sam was still holding the notebook, her curiosity almost too much to bear as she found her fingers eager to flip open the pages. She turned her attention back to the detective and the scene before her that resembled a shoot at "Life of the Rich and Famous." "What's the story about the cat? If Jane can travel around in time, what does she need Floppy for?"

Montmart's gray eyebrows quirked, but he seemed in a better mood now than after they'd discussed his wife. "It might be her Familiar. If you believe the time-travel story, you might as well believe that Oldsfield's a witch. Halloween will be here soon enough."

Sam looked at the yellowing tips of some of the trees along the winding drive up to the house and agreed but not about the witch theory. She knew he wasn't serious about that. "The cat has to serve a purpose. Greg said she's using it as a Guinea Pig for the project. He also said Floppy acts like a grounder, so Jane is able to switch places with him in different times. Maybe that's all here in this book."

"I wouldn't put much weight into that," the detective warned. "She's encouraging you to read it, despite her warnings not to show it to the police. I doubt there's anything of value in it. It's what we call in police jargon, "a ruse.""

"Then why are you taking me to your house?"

Montmart was parked near the front door. This close, Sam could see the house was more a work of art than a building. The white was pristine, as if it had been recently painted. Doric columns, designed in the Grecian style, flanked the entryway.

There were even actual statues planted in key spots along the wide verandah.

Seeing her reaction, Montmart answered the question in her mind and not the one she'd just asked. "You ain't seen nothin yet, honey. The inside is an interior decorator's dream while the gardens out back are a landscaper's fantasy." Montmart turned off the car's ignition and unbuckled his seat belt. "The reason I'm asking you to come to my house," he emphasized the word 'asking' as opposed to 'taking' "is for your safety; not because I'm in a rush to read that book." He glanced down at the notebook in Sam's lap, and she got the impression that was an excuse to look up and down her legs. She wondered how long the lascivious detective had been widowed and whether he'd been a flirt throughout his marriage.

"I can take care of myself," she said, unconsciously pulling down her skirt.

He didn't comment. Instead, he opened the car door and started walking toward the house. When she didn't immediately follow, he turned back and asked, "Who are you waiting for, Robin Leach?"

Sam was growing angrier with the detective, but she didn't know why his attitude was bothering her so much. She usually didn't let people ruffle her that way. She joined him at the solid oak door. There was a concealed alarm unit above and to the right of the golden lion's head doorknob. Montmart expertly found the panel and disarmed it with such a quick succession of keystrokes that Sam had no idea which numbers he'd used.

"You first," he said after he'd opened the door to the darkened entry hall.

Sam slid in ahead of him, half expecting him to pat her on the rear. If he was protecting her, who was protecting her from him?

Sam adjusted her eyes to the darkness of the interior. It looked as if it hadn't been lived in recently. As she tried to make out the rooms in front of her, the detective hit a light switch from below the wall sconces and illuminated the scene. And what a scene it was! The house's interior was simple but ornate. An uncluttered menagerie of fine art, probably authentic, amid gilded furniture and walls of painted murals and damask tapestries. The entry hall, which Sam estimated was larger than her bedroom, had no furnishings except for a bronze settee where weary guests could rest and gaze upon the lavish setting. Looking up, Sam saw a tiled ceiling in a pattern of gold leaves and pearlescent marble. She felt heady from the aesthetics and almost wanted to take a seat on the bronze bench but forced herself to walk ahead into the sunken living room where bright gold was again the dominant color.

Montmart followed her like a puppy let off its leash to wander after its master. "The sunroom is this way," he said from behind her. Sam turned and saw him walk toward French doors to the right. Beyond, she saw the late afternoon daylight filtering in, bathing the wood floor covered with an Oriental carpet in burnished shades of copper. She joined the detective, who was looking out on an enclosed gazebo-like porch that contained wicker chairs and pots of exotic green plants, which Sam knew she wouldn't be able to pronounce, even if she knew their names. A botanist she was not.

Philip slid the glass door to the left and walked out. He hadn't invited Sam ahead this time, nor had he asked her to follow. She wondered why until she noticed he was crouching and then saw what he was after. Seated on one of the wicker chairs was the familiar gray cat.

Sam tiptoed after the detective so as not to disturb the feline. She found the man's movements comical, as he got down on the cat's level and reached out a hand to pet him. "Here, Kitty, Kitty."

The cat was rolled in a hefty gray ball, eyelids shut in sleep. When Montmart touched him, he opened his right eye to reveal a narrow, yellow slit.

"He's awake," Sam whispered. "Are you going to question him?"

The detective kept his eye on the cat and his position on the tiled floor immobile. "No," he replied in a matching whisper that sounded like sandpaper being lightly brushed. "I want to catch him and bring him back with us."

Both eyes were open now as the cat stretched out his white front paws, raised his head, and yawned, revealing a pink mouth full of sharp incisors inherited from his wilder relatives.

"I don't know if that's a good idea. Jane seems to be able to cast him back in time whenever she wants."

Montmart continued petting the cat slowly, as he edged closer intent on the capture. "She's just a good magician, Sam. I want to find out where her strings are. The cat could be the key."

Before Sam could say another word, the detective stood up, reached out, and swept the cat into his arms. There was a brief struggle but not a serious one, as the animal adjusted itself to its new location. "Fat cat," Montmart remarked in a breathless voice that was back to its normal pitch.

Sam noticed the gray fur that floated off Floppy as he vacated the chair. A bunch of it settled down on the wicker seat passing through some of the holes to gather on the floor below. "He seems to be shedding, too," she remarked.

Montmart carried the cat back into the house. "C'mon, Sam, let's get out of here. I want to get this kitty into my car before he realizes I'm catnapping him."

"Can't be worse than what Oldsfield's been doing to him." Sam followed behind the feline-toting detective as he made his way through the beautiful home. She caught only passing glimpses of the rooms on the way out. Sam considered it close to a miracle, but Montmart made it to his car without a scratch. The only time the cat even shifted in his arms was when Philip reset the alarm after Sam came through the front door behind him.

"Now's the tricky part," the detective said as he arrived at his car. "I have to hand him to you, so I can open the doors. In fact, I need you to sit him on your lap while I drive."

"I think I can manage that." Sam walked over to the detective and opened her arms for the hefty delivery. Floppy wasn't unduly upset by the change, but cried as he was being handed over to Sam.

"Now, Floppy boy, stay calm," Sam said in her best feline-pleasing voice. "You're a bit heavier than Holly, but I think I can keep a grip on you."

The cat quieted down, and Sam steadied him on her lap after the detective let her and their furry passenger into his Toyota. In order to do so, though, she had to move the notebook to the floor by her feet.

"I'll take that," the detective offered getting in beside her and placing the notebook behind him in the back seat. He started the car, and Floppy cried again at the sudden noise. Sam recalled reading in one of her cat magazines that a cat's vocabulary consists of a variety of sounds that have different meanings. The meow Floppy made when the engine revved sounded more fearful than the one he made when Philip had given him over to her.

"Don't be afraid, boy," Sam said stroking the cat's silky gray fur. "We're just taking a little ride." She noticed Montmart wasn't lighting up nor turning on his favorite country station and wondered if it was because he didn't want to upset the cat whose senses were more acute than their own. The radio would probably sound as loud and maybe more grinding to Floppy's delicate ears than the car's motor, as the cigarette smoke would smell even more acrid to his keen nose. It seemed the detective was much better at handling animals than people and was more concerned with his impression on them, as well. That was a shame because, even though Sam was still wary with the man, she found she wanted to trust him.

Floppy calmed down on the ride to Montmart's house, which took less than ten minutes. Although the detective didn't live in such an opulent nor isolated neighborhood as Jane Oldsfield, his house was nothing to sniff at. Sam again wondered where his money had come from and why he'd chosen to remain in the house where his wife had been murdered if that's where the murder had taken place.

When the detective pulled into the curving driveway that was bordered by neat topiary hedges, Sam felt a trickle of fear spread through her. The cat, sensing her uneasiness, stiffened in her lap alert for signs of danger. There were none. The scene was a quiet, serene picture of a ranch home with several additions in an upper-class area on Long Island. Although it was framed in gray clouds, which were now draping across the suddenly darkened sky, it was otherwise an innocent panorama. Sam didn't know whether she was expecting Jane to jump out in front of the car waving her time-travel disk or the witch's broom that Philip had hypothesized. In either case, her senses were as heightened as the cat's.

The split ranch had a new-looking dormer on top that Sam imagined had been added in the last couple of years. The house, itself, was sided in pale yellow aluminum with white trim. While well kept, it wasn't a new house. Most of the homes she'd seen on the streets around the detective's were in the forty to fifty-year ranges, Sam judged.

Montmart parked the car and gathered up the notebook. Sam realized he was leaving Floppy in her hands, literally. "Welcome to my casa," he said, and Sam was surprised it was the Spanish word for home he used instead of the French.

Sam got out with Floppy squirming in her arms. Now that they had arrived at their destination, the cat had decided to try to make his escape. Sam had to hold him tight as she dragged the furry lug into the house.

The interior of Montmart's home took Sam by surprise. Where Jane's house had conveyed a light, almost ethereal quality, Philip's was dark and shadowed. The walls were paneled in a deep Maple, while the furnishings were black and gray. It made the place appear smaller but not cozier. Sam shivered as a cold draft passed through the door as she stepped through the entrance. Montmart, taking this for a sign of difficulty with the cat, told her she could put the animal down as he closed the door behind them.

The chill didn't pass as Sam lowered Floppy to the ground and walked into the living room. The cat, free of his captor, ran to hide under the black leather sofa. Sam had never liked the modern look for decor, so she found the room she'd entered distasteful. In addition, it was a mess. There were newspapers, magazines, and other recyclable material strewn about the slate carpet. She caught a glimpse of a few copies of *Playboy* amid the pile that featured mainly news publications.

Montmart didn't seem embarrassed by neither the state of his house nor by the evidence of his recreational reading habits. He ignored the papers by stepping around them and put the notebook he carried in with him on the couch as he took a seat.

"Sit down, Sam. The cat will come out in due time. I want to get started on this right away."

Sam hadn't expected an escorted tour of the house but thought the detective would've at least offered her a drink or a bite to eat before diving into work. Although disappointed at his lack of manners as a host, she took a seat next to the notebook, which served as a divider between them. As she sat, the distant bark of a dog came from somewhere at the back of the house. It was then that she remembered the pit bulls.

"Sounds like Rover wants to say hello."

"Don't worry about him. He's in his kennel in the backyard. I'll introduce you later." The detective passed her the notebook as he flicked on a light that sat on the hexagonal end table next to the couch. "We have a lot of reading to do."

Sam reached over and turned on the matching light at her side of the couch. "Shouldn't we start toward the back where all the information is and read the beginning at another time?"

Montmart didn't seem happy with this approach. "I think we should begin at the beginning, and it'll save eyestrain if we alternate reading."

"Since I'm holding the notebook, I might as well read first,"

Sam said. She was about to open the book when she remembered Mr. Clancy. He was probably waiting for her at the apartment now. "Before we begin, can I use your phone? I have to make arrangements for those plans I had for tonight."

Montmart sounded angry. "All right but make it fast. The phone's in the bedroom. I only have one now. I disconnected the other because I don't like being disturbed when I work. If the phone rings back there, it doesn't bother me as much." When Sam looked at him questioningly, he added, "The bedroom's down the hall. Last room on the right."

"Thanks. I won't be long." But just to make sure he didn't peek she brought the notebook with her. She passed several closed doors on her way to the bedroom but found one open. Entering, she came upon a brighter, softer room with cream walls and a queen-sized feather bed. The room seemed bare. Not as if it had yet to be decorated but as if some previous decorations had been removed. Walking to the telephone on the small bed stand near the window, Sam saw a framed photograph of a woman with long red hair a shade lighter than her own and laughing blue eyes. She was dressed in a denim jumper holding a basket of wildflowers. If this was Philip's wife, RoseAnn, why was the only picture he seemed to have of her one that didn't include him? It was odd that the wedding photo wasn't on display, but she thought it might be hidden behind one of the closed doors she'd passed on her way down the hall.

Picking up the phone, Sam dialed Angie, hoping her friend was home. On the second ring, Angie answered.

"Angie Palmer speaking."

"Angie, it's Sam. I'm still on Long Island. I need you to do me a favor." The words came out in one long breath.

"Sam? Are you okay? You're not still at the meeting with Parsons, are you?"

"No, and I'm fine. It's just that I'm taking care of something else." She almost lied and said she was at her mother's. Instead, she continued at the same hasty pace. "Can you go to my apartment and feed Holly? Also, I promised John Clancy I'd make him a spaghetti dinner tonight. Can you tell him I've been delayed and pick up some Italian food for him or take him out to dinner? I'll pay you back."

Angie didn't reply right away, and Sam was afraid she'd turn her down. She should've known her friend better.

"Sure, Sam. Don't worry. I still have the extra key you gave me for cat sitting the last time you went away. You told me to keep it in case of an emergency, and I guess this is one."

Sam let out a sigh of relief. "I really appreciate that, Angie. I owe you one. I gotta go. I'll call you as soon as I get home."

Sam replaced the phone on the receiver and was about to get off the bed when she heard footsteps coming down the hall toward her – Philip Montmart's footsteps. *Great. Just what I need, a sex-maniac detective joining me in his bedroom.* She leapt off the bed so hard that she nearly catapulted into the unlit fireplace on the opposite end of the room. Nice touch, bedroom fireplace, too bad he didn't decorate the rest of the house to match. But maybe she'd decorated the bedroom. Sam looked again at the picture of the pretty woman who'd been married for an indeterminate number of years to the chain-smoking detective and wondered how long ago she'd been killed and how. Had it been in this house? In this room? She shivered involuntarily and almost jumped out of her shoes when Montmart entered.

"Sorry to scare you. I wanted to let you know that I need to feed the dogs now. Then, if you're hungry, I'll make us some dinner. The notebook can wait a little longer. I'd rather we don't stop once we begin reading it."

"That sounds logical."

"What do you know about pit bulls, Sam?"

Sam was taken aback by the question. She felt uncomfortable sitting on the bed, so she got up and stood by the detective at the entrance to the room. "I've never owned one if that's what you're asking. I've always been a cat person, but I have nothing against dogs. I've heard some bad things about pit bulls, though." She was trying to edge around Montmart to escape into the hall.

"They can be very dangerous," he said. "Some people train them improperly. Mine are attack dogs. I breed them for that purpose and that purpose only."

Sam didn't like the sound of his voice. There was a hard edge to it. Rough gravel, hard as cement. She wanted to change the subject, but he seemed insistent on continuing.

"I started breeding the dogs after my wife was killed in case the killers came back. Not to save myself but to rip them to shreds."

Sam didn't want to hear this. She didn't want to stand in the doorway with this man she hardly knew listening to his plans for revenge.

"You've probably wondered why a man of my income lives in a house like this," he went on ignoring the look of unease on her face. "I married money. RoseAnn came from a wealthy family. She married me against her father's wishes, but her mother convinced him not to disinherit her. The money was never an issue with me, though. We could've lived like paupers, and I'd have loved her no less."

The gravel was breaking up, the cement cracking. Sam heard the sadness in his voice. She wouldn't know what to do if he started crying, but she sensed he was stronger than that, or at least, he put on a good show.

He turned back toward the hall. "I'd like you to see them. You might as well while you're here. Don't worry. They're trained on command."

Sam followed Montmart to a back door that led out into the kennel area. There were half a dozen wire cages there with a dog in each.

"They all need their own space," he explained answering her unasked question. He went over to the cage with the largest dog and showed the animal a bag Sam hadn't realized he was holding. "Chow time, Rover," he said. Then he turned back to his guest. "I'm going to open his cage. Just stay where you are. He's very well behaved."

Sam nearly laughed at the thought that she might try to move if he'd asked her to. Rover was entirely black with sharp teeth he was baring as he recognized the food bag.

Montmart took a keychain out of his pocket and opened Rover's kennel. Slipping inside, he fed the dog some meat scraps by hand. Sam was amazed at how obedient the animal seemed. After allowing Rover his ration of food, Montmart locked up the kennel and went on to the next. He repeated this ritual until each dog was fed and then came back to Sam.

"I feed them twice a day. In the morning and around the time I eat dinner. I prefer meat to dog food. It keeps their teeth sharp."

Sam was starting to think she should call a cab back to Manhattan and leave the detective/dog trainer to his journal reading.

"Are you hungry?" he asked as he opened the door back into the house.

"Not anymore."

Montmart laughed. "I promise I won't make steak. I was thinking of baking some chicken breasts."

"Delicious." Sam's tone was sarcastic as she followed the detective down the hall and toward the kitchen she hadn't seen yet.

This room also had the marks of a woman's touch. The walls were covered in homey brick with old-fashioned hanging copper molds and pans. The fading sunlight shone through large plate glass windows that bathed the warm room in a soft, golden hue. This seemed to be where meals were eaten as well as prepared because there was a round maple wood table with six matching chairs with French legs to the left of the modern cooking area that was a pleasing contrast to the antique furniture. The stove, under-cabinet microwave, dishwasher, and side-by-side refrigerator were all a light brown with black trim. The cabinets, which had a new antique look, were the same shade of Maple as the kitchen table and chair.

"This was RoseAnn's favorite room," Montmart said from beside her. "We used to cook dinner together occasionally. She insisted on making our own meals, even though we could've afforded a cook." He walked over to the refrigerator and took out a package of Perdue chicken breasts. "I'll get these started. You can have a seat if you'd like."

Sam felt a bit foolish standing there while the detective began arranging spices from the revolving spice rack on the counter next to the toaster. "I used to get takeout most nights after work because it seemed like a waste cooking for one person, but I can manage a reasonable home-cooked meal."

Sam felt obligated to ask if he wanted her help, although she was afraid he'd take her up on it and invite her to assist him as his wife had. Instead, he said, "I never got in RoseAnn's way, but I know my way around this place a lot better than you do. Sit down and relax. It won't take long."

Sam watched Montmart as he went about the dinner preparations. She sat in one of the kitchen chairs that she hoped hadn't been his wife's. After the detective finished slicing and dicing the side-dish vegetables and had put the layered chicken casserole into the oven to bake, he placed a salad bowl in front of her and another before the seat across from her. He filled the salad bowl with mixed greens and a few cucumbers and tomatoes.

"You can start on that if you'd like. The chicken should be ready in about a half hour."

"I can wait a bit longer."

"So can I." Montmart sat across from her. "Sorry, there's no dressing. I forgot to get some this week. I don't eat salad that often."

Sam was thinking about Mr. Clancy and wondering if Angie was eating with him now. A feeling of guilt took hold of her, but she nudged it off. She was working, not playing. "You really didn't have to go to so much trouble. A sandwich would've been fine."

Montmart shrugged. "I always try to have at least one full meal a day. There was a time when I wasn't eating at all. I existed on tobacco, and it did a number on my stomach. I almost got an ulcer."

Sam assumed he was referring to the period after his wife's death. She was curious about it but was afraid to ask about the details. It was better if he came around with the story on his own. "Have you lived here by yourself a long time?" she asked, phrasing the question to deliberately exclude mention of RoseAnn.

Montmart seemed to have a change in heart, or of stomach, as he lifted a forkful of lettuce, tomato, and cucumber onto his plate. Looking down at his salad, he replied, "It was nine months last week." He picked up his knife and fork and began cutting the lettuce into pieces. There was silence between them except for the sound of the knife's blade shredding the lettuce. Then he looked up at her and, changing the subject abruptly, said, "If the notebook takes us too long to finish tonight, I think you should stay here. You have to be back at Virtual Software tomorrow again, anyway. And I presume you made provisions for your cat."

Sam was glad she hadn't begun eating her salad because she was sure she would've choked. "Yes. I called my friend and asked her to feed Holly, but I can't stay here tonight. If you don't want to bring me back into the city, I could take transportation or stay at a hotel."

"Why should you do that? There's lots of room here, and it would be very safe. The dogs will let me know if anyone comes near the place, unless they walk through walls as Oldsfield wants us to believe she does."

"Thanks for the offer, but I'd rather not." She didn't add that she was more afraid of him than Jane Oldsfield at the moment.

Montmart lifted his fork to his mouth and chewed the salad slowly before swallowing. "Okay. Let me know if you change your mind." He got up to check the chicken and turn the casserole. When he came back to the table, Sam was munching on some lettuce. The smell of baking chicken had awakened her appetite. It had also brought Floppy out from hiding into the kitchen. He jumped up on the table without preamble and gave Sam a look that was a combination of begging and demanding. "Hey, guess who's joining us for dinner?" she said. Then to the cat, "For a time-traveling feline, you sure didn't bring any table manners back from any of your journeys." She picked him up and placed him on the floor just as Montmart served the main dish.

During dinner, they shared idle small talk that didn't touch again on Montmart's deceased wife or his offer for Sam to spend the night. She found the meal tasty as the light talk continued. She fed some table scraps to Floppy who waited patiently by her seat gobbling up each piece of chicken before she had time to offer the next. When the cat's appetite was finally sated, he walked back into the living room, curled up on the couch, and went to sleep.

It was only when Sam got up to help the detective clear the table and load the dishes into the dishwasher that another sensitive subject was raised.

"I'd like to get started on the notebook as soon as possible," Montmart said. He looked over to the opposite end of the kitchen table where Sam had laid it during dinner.

"That's fine with me. Where will we be reading?" She hoped his answer wasn't the bedroom and was relieved when he led the way toward the living room.

Montmart took his previous seat on the couch, while Sam took the one by the lamp. The only change from their first positions was that the cat now lay between them. Montmart didn't seem to care either way. He was lighting up an after-dinner cigarette.

"Can you please go easy on those things? I was thankful you didn't smoke at the kitchen table, but I might start choking if I have to read with all that secondhand smoke around me."

"Pardon me." The detective stubbed out the cigarette in a nearby ashtray. Sam noticed there were several of them in the area with numerous butts in them similar to the ones in his car. "I'll try to hold off. I've probably met my quota for the day, anyhow."

"I'd say." Sam opened the notebook to the first page. The cat beside her was purring, so she had to raise her voice above the motor. The dark handwriting on the page was neat and very legible. It was dated November 1, 1997, nearly a year ago.

This is the first page of what will be a recording of a very special project. Although I'll try to keep the technical details at a minimum, I'm keeping this journal as my own report of the project.

My partner and I, Greg Parsons, were experimenting with a new microchip device housed in a hand-held computer that I designed. The original concept was for a virtual travel program that had the potential to revolutionize current transportation systems. Initial tests on this program included sending objects short distances. We tried manipulating pens, paper clips, coins, and similar items from a foot to several yards away. The results of these trials were successful. Yet, when we attempted to move these same objects greater distances, the objects couldn't be located. It was assumed the settings for distances beyond certain perimeters were faulty. Further tests on larger objects will be conducted to substantiate these findings.

Sam paused. "Should I continue reading?"

Montmart had begun stroking the cat, but his attention seemed focused on Sam. It made her feel uncomfortable, even though she knew it was only his interest in the journal that was causing that intent stare.

"Yes. Don't stop until you're tired."

The next entry was dated a week later and the following ones at varying intervals from a few days to months apart so that Sam knew the records hadn't been kept on a daily basis, but that Jane had written in the journal only when significant occurrences had taken place, like a diarist recording the highlights of her life and leaving out the mundane day-to-day events.

November 8, 1997

Although we've made some progress in sending larger objects further distances, we're discovering that the settings on the Travel Disk are incorrect. When two items are sent with the same coordinates, they're not arriving at the same destination. Greg believes the size of the objects is affecting where they are being transported. However, we've still not ascertained where some of the objects are traveling, as we can't locate many of the items that are sent. I've suggested using some live subjects such as mice, but Greg is resistant to this idea. He believes we should perfect the sending of inanimate objects before we experiment with live ones. I disagree with him and may try some experiments on my own.

November 20, 1997

Last night, I stayed at the office late after Greg went home. I tried sending a white mouse across the room. I'd gotten the rodent from one of my friends at the University science department. I charmed him into letting me use "Pygmy" on the condition that I'd go out with him to a movie this weekend. If I make Greg jealous, I don't care. He could use a little shaking up. He's so damned serious and ethical about everything. By the way, the mouse disappeared, but the odd thing is that a vase I'd tried sending down the hall last week appeared in the same spot Pygmy was supposed to arrive.

Sam paused. "It seems Jane must have had a thing going with Greg Parsons, and what do you make of the mouse and vase switch?"

When Montmart didn't answer, she looked up from the notebook. The detective was no longer staring at her, nor was he petting the cat. He was leaned back against a pillow with his eyes closed.

Sam couldn't believe it. He'd been wide awake a moment

ago. Her first impulse was to shake him, but then he started to snore. It was a low humming sound not too different from a cat's purr that rippled from his chest through his nose and from his mouth.

Great! He's asleep on the job again and snoring, she thought. *Just like when I was expecting him to monitor me when I was talking with Parsons. Only then his country music station had lulled him to bye bye land.* She didn't blame him for that because country music always bored her to tears. On the other hand, his nodding off at the sound of her voice didn't please her. But if she woke him now, would he be in any capacity to drive her home? She considered calling a taxi and making a silent getaway, but some strange impulse made her quietly rise from the couch and leave the sleeping investigator and the cat to their dreams. She found herself with the notebook under her arm walking back down the hall toward the room Montmart had shared with his wife. She decided that if he awoke before she fell asleep, they'd continue their reading. If not, she would stay the night, fully dressed, on top of the covers, with the lights on, aware of every sound including the dogs outside and Jane Oldsfield's laugh if she decided to pay another unwanted visit. But especially aware of the detective's footsteps if he should awaken and come looking for her.

CHAPTER THIRTEEN

"The road was new to me, as roads always are, going back."

— SARA ORNE JEWETT 1849-1909 THE COUNTRY OF
POINTED FIRS [1896], CHAPTER 5

Sam awoke with a slight headache and a vague feeling of fear. She was lying on the covers of an unfamiliar feather bed wearing yesterday's dress. Outside, she heard the light tap of raindrops and the low growl of dogs. Somewhere down the hall, she smelled coffee brewing.

Remembering where she was, she jumped to her feet and ran to the window. Montmart was by the kennels feeding the dogs. He wore a yellow rain slicker, even though the rain was steady but not yet heavy. He either heard her or sensed that she'd awakened, because he turned toward the window when she appeared and gave her a crooked smile. A few minutes later, he stood outside the bedroom door with a few raindrops falling from his jacket sleeves. His wet hair looked darker and a lot less gray.

"Good morning. Sorry I fell asleep on you, but I was exhausted. I haven't been sleeping well lately. In fact, that was the best sleep I've had in a long time."

Sam felt awkward in her mussed dress and unbrushed hair. She was in dire need of a shower but was afraid to ask.

"I'm guilty of the same crime. I didn't realize how tired I was yesterday, either."

"What time is it?"

"Almost ten. I didn't want to wake you, but I made another pot of coffee just in case you got up on your own. I've already been through a pot myself."

"Ten O'clock! That doesn't leave us much time. You haven't read the book without me, have you?"

Montmart grinned. He almost looked boyish. "No. I've been thinking it over, and I think we should change our tactics this time."

Sam wasn't comfortable standing beside him in the doorway. She made an excuse to escape. "You do? Well, you can tell me all your ideas in the kitchen. I really can use that cup of coffee."

The detective let her slip by as she made her way to the rustic dining area. When she entered the kitchen, she noticed Floppy eating hungrily from a small bowl on the floor.

"I fed him before I went out to the dogs. He was quite persistent. Good thing I still had some cat food cans in the house."

Sam went to the coffee machine and poured the hot liquid into one of the white mugs on the counter. "Want another cup?" she offered.

"No, thanks. But we can split the box of Hostess Donuts," he said referring to the package of assorted frosted, chocolate, and cinnamon covered cakes on the table.

Sam added milk from the nearby pitcher to her coffee and brought it over to the table. Montmart had taken the same seat from the night before, and she followed suit again, taking the chair across from him. Floppy, satisfied by his own breakfast, ambled away.

"So," the detective began opening the donut box and taking out one of the white sugar powdered ones. "The new plan is to go back to Parsons. This time, however, I'll accompany you. That scene yesterday at your sister's was very strange. I don't have much patience, and I can't wait much longer to get to the bottom of this." Although Montmart was referring to the current situation, Sam couldn't help but think there was a second meaning to his words.

"What did you get from the part you heard me read last night?" she asked sipping her coffee. Her stomach wasn't in the mood for donuts.

The powder had rubbed off on Montmart's upper lip giving him a white moustache. "The books are a fabrication. Oldsfield is leading us on. This whole time travel business is a cover up for something else. She's either in on it herself, or he's in on it with her. I tend to think the latter is the case. I don't trust either of them."

Sam didn't think Philip Montmart trusted many people, but maybe he had a reason. "I know you're pretty fixed on your view of this, but suppose Jane and Greg are telling the truth? What then?"

The detective wiped his mouth with a napkin. "Have you been to Disney World, Sam?"

The strange reply took her by surprise. She almost choked on her coffee. "My sister and I went when we were kids when there was only the Magic Kingdom before Epcot and MGM were built. Jennifer loved it. It was her kind of place. She cried when we left. She said she wanted to live there and even tried running away from home afterwards. Mom found her at the airport trying to buy tickets to Orlando with Monopoly money. That was when Dad was still alive, and Mom only saw doctors when she was sick."

"But what did you think of Disney?" Montmart persisted.

"It was fun. I remember the castle, seeing it all lit up at night. I knew I wasn't Cinderella, though. I knew it was only an expensive fantasy that I would have to leave when our vacation was through."

"Exactly." Montmart's light blue eyes were shining. His hair was drying into gray curls around his head. "For someone who can tell the difference between fantasy and reality, you sure are having a hard time with this Virtual Software story. There's no supposing, Sam. The story is false. Period."

She didn't want to argue with him. "If you say so, but before we go back to Parsons, I think I should call Jennifer and make sure Jane hasn't paid her another visit. I also have to call Angie and ask her to check on my cat again."

"Fine. I'll be out in the car taking a smoke. Meet me there when you're ready. Oh, and by the way," he looked her up and down in that way that made her feel like a streetwalker, "there's a change of clothes in the bedroom closet. My wife was about your size. If you want a quick shower, you can take that, too. And don't forget Floppy when you're done. He's coming with us."

Sam should've questioned the clothes and the shower, but she knew she needed them both. Instead, she asked about the cat. "What do you intend to do with Floppy?"

Montmart shrugged. "I don't know yet, but I'll figure it out. If he's Parsons' cat, he'll be glad to be reunited with him."

When Montmart left, Sam made her calls. Jennifer hadn't seen Jane again, but she told Sam that their mother had gone to another doctor because she didn't believe Dr. Carter's diagnosis that there was nothing wrong with her. Angie sounded upset that Sam wasn't home yet. She said Holly and Mr. Clancy were both fine and had been well fed (Clancy with an Italian dinner from John's Pizzeria on Bleecker Street). Angie was worried about Sam and told her to be careful. That frightened Sam even more because her friend was far from the play-it-safe type.

After Sam took a quick shower, she put on a sunflower print blouse and matching skirt that she found in RoseAnn's closet. It fit her perfectly, which made her feel guiltier. Even though the detective had suggested it, she was afraid of how he would feel seeing her in the outfit. Or was she afraid of wearing it?

Catching Floppy was another ordeal. As soon as he saw her coming, he darted under the couch. No amount of cajoling would coax him out until she baited him by opening another cat food can she found in the kitchen. When he slinked out of his hiding place to devour the morsels, Sam grabbed him and carried him out to the car along with the notebook she clutched in her other hand.

Montmart was sitting in his car listening to his favorite country music station puffing on what was probably his tenth cigarette. He smiled at her as she hefted the cat inside, and she felt angry that he hadn't even opened the car door for her.

"Good going. I trust everything is set for our expedition."

Sam replied in a clipped tone, "Thanks to me, I guess it is. What do you plan on telling Parsons?"

"The truth. I'm sick of beating around the bush. I want to see what's inside it." He glanced at her again with that disconcerting glance. "That looks nice on you. It was one of RoseAnn's favorites."

Sam gulped back a thank you. She didn't want to tread on thin ice. Floppy was becoming slippery on her lap. "If Parsons really is in on this, and if it's camouflaging something illegal, as you think it is, won't the truth be dangerous?"

Montmart revved the engine. "Could be, but I'm prepared for that."

"What does that mean?"

"There's a 45 in the glove box. I don't like carrying it on me all the time, but I make exceptions when I think a situation calls for it."

Sam gasped. Floppy, sensing her surprise, almost jumped off her lap. "Are you serious? If you are, then you can go meet Parsons yourself. I don't like being in the middle of a shooting match."

The detective's voice was flat. "I don't blame you. If you'd prefer, you can wait in the car. But I promise you that I'll take the utmost precautions if you come along." Then he added in almost a whisper, "I'll never endanger another person's life again."

CHAPTER FOURTEEN

"We all have our time machines. Some take us back, they're called memories. Some take us forward, they're called dreams.

— JEREMY IRONS

M ontmart parked in Virtual Software's parking lot behind the glass-fronted building. He got out first and went around to open the passenger side door. Sam hadn't expected this and felt thankful when he also volunteered to carry Floppy. He left the notebook toting to her.

Floppy, reacting to a sense of deja vu aka feline instinct, seemed to know he was on his way home to his owner. He hardly complained except for a low meow when the detective transferred him from Sam's arms to his.

It was late morning and the smell of coffee brewing for breaks was wafting from office doors on either side of the entranceway. The secretaries and businessmen who they passed on their way to the elevator didn't glance twice at them even though they looked conspicuously like a pair of catnappers with an agenda.

When they arrived at Virtual Software, Parsons answered the

door on the first knock as if he was waiting for them. Again, there was no evidence of his receptionist. Today he was dressed more informally in beige slacks and a cream pullover sweater that emphasized the breadth of his upper body. The sight of him made Sam almost forget the gun Montmart was carrying.

Parsons didn't seem surprised to see Montmart nor his cat. The latter puzzled Sam more. As soon as the door opened, Greg ushered them inside with a jovial smile. "Glad you could make it," he said without making eye contact with either of them. "And thanks for bringing Floppy. I just put out his favorite cat food in a bowl."

Montmart sidestepped Sam and entered first, letting the cat jump from his hands onto the floor by Parsons' feet. Floppy recognized him immediately and began purring as the tall man bent down to pet his head.

"Touching reunion," the detective commented. "And since you've traveled ahead in time, you probably know who I am."

Parsons looked up. "Yes. You're Detective Philip Montmart, and you're going to give me a hell of a time proving that I'm telling the truth."

Montmart didn't look impressed. "Psychics use psychology; magicians use props. I just need to find your trick."

Floppy, either sensing an ensuing argument or sniffing his food, backed away toward the inner office. Greg stood his ground between Montmart and Sam.

"I have no trick, Detective, but I do have proof. I know you'll believe me eventually, although you don't think that now."

There was a pause as the two men eyed one another as if preparing for a duel that Sam sincerely hoped wouldn't occur. She doubted that the short detective would be any match for the tall, muscular programmer in a physical fight, but she had a feeling Montmart would be the victor of a shootout.

"So, why don't you show me this proof?" Philip challenged. "Send me back in time. In fact, I'll tell you when and where I'd like to go, December 20th of last year at my house around two in the afternoon. I should've been there that day, but I was on a case. Another ruined weekend, my wife said. She'd stay home and finish decorating the Christmas tree. I never saw her again. One of the bastards I put away took their revenge on me, and I don't even know who did it." His voice was beginning to crack, and the feverish look was back in his eyes. "Send me back there, Parsons, and I'll believe you. Otherwise, you better tell me the rules to whatever game you're playing."

"I knew you'd ask me to do that," Parsons said. "And I will, but it's going to be dangerous. You're not going to be able to save her, you know. That would change time irrevocably. The only thing you'll be able to do is witness the act. Are you sure that's what you want to do? It'll be like a movie. You'll see her killer, but you won't be able to catch him. Of course, once you know who he is, you'll be able to bring that information back with you to exact whatever vendetta you have in mind if the killer is still around. Do you understand? Do you still wish to proceed?"

"I don't understand anything, but that's fine. Beam me up, Scottie, or whatever you do."

"You'll need a Time-Travel Disk. I can't set it exactly, but I can get you pretty close to the day and time – maybe a bit earlier but not later. Samantha should go with you. I have to stay here." He turned and called back to them. "Follow me into my office and I'll set you both up. I can program your return settings into the disk also. Your stay will be limited. Fifteen minutes at the most. The shorter the length of time, the more accurate the transport will be."

Parsons led them through the reception room to his office where the first thing they saw was Floppy slurping up food from a blue plastic bowl next to the desk.

"You're actually damn good," Montmart said, looking up at Parsons and trying to talk down to him at the same time.

Greg ignored the comment and went around to his desk

drawer where he extracted one of the compass-like objects Sam was now familiar with.

"It's tricky sending two people back to the same time and place. You'll have to hold hands around the time-travel disk. It doesn't hurt. In fact, it's nothing like you've probably imagined. Your particles don't fizzle into thin air like in the Star Trek shows, nor do you board a time machine like the one in the "Back to the Future" movies. It'll be, more or less, instantaneous." He turned toward Sam. "If he tries to stop the murder or interfere with the past in any way, you have to push the center button on the disk. It'll abort the transport immediately and bring you both back. Do you understand?"

Sam didn't understand, but she merely nodded and asked as she placed the notebook down on his desk, "Do we both have to hold hands around the disk to return?"

"No, only to leave. I suggest, though, that you hold the disk after you arrive at your destination. It's very important."

Sam heard laughter and turned to see the detective smiling. The scar in his cheek was wrinkling as the laugh lines appeared around his blue eyes like tiny islands dotting the ocean. "You're taking this pretty far, aren't you, Parsons? You really believe you're going to send me back to witness my wife's murder. I underestimated you. You're not just a con man, you're an insane con man. What's in that disk, anyway? Have you hidden any explosives that'll detonate when we grab it?"

"You've been watching too many spy thrillers, Detective. This disk actually houses a very sophisticated computer with a special microchip that enables time travel. It took Jane and me years to design it, and even then, we weren't aware of its full potential or danger." He walked over to Montmart and handed him the disk, then took Sam's hand and placed it on top. "If there was a bomb in this, I wouldn't stand so close. Don't move. The settings will activate in three seconds. When you return, you'll be back in this room three seconds later, even though you'll have spent more time back in the past."

. . .

The last thing Sam remembered was the clock behind Greg, a digital pendulum which was a modern version of a grandfather clock. It read one o'clock and was beeping its digital chimes. On the second beep, she was no longer in the room. Instead, she and Philip were standing in front of a house that looked very similar to his home in Old Brookville, only the front door and windows were decorated with wreaths, garland, and adhesive snowflakes. It wasn't yet dark, but it felt later in the afternoon.

"My God!" Montmart exclaimed. "Has he drugged us? That's my house. That's how she decorated it last year before ... before I threw everything away." His voice sounded hoarser than its usual deepness. He still gripped her hand. Somehow, Sam remembered to take the disk away from him, and he let her hand fall free as she released it. She felt like a traitor.

Philip walked toward the house. Sam followed automatically. She saw lights on in the front room and the outline of a woman passing before the windows.

"It can't be," Montmart murmured as if to himself. Then he took off, running toward the door. Sam wanted to call after him, but she knew that no matter how loud she yelled, he wouldn't hear her. He was emotionally, as well as physically, back in time.

As Sam caught up with him on the doorstep, the outline of the woman became clearer, but there was another outline in the house, too. The killer was already there. Sam knew she shouldn't let Montmart enter. Parsons said he could watch but couldn't interfere. She reached out and touched the detective's arm gently. "Please, Philip," she said calling him by the first name she hardly used, even though he allowed it. "Stay here."

The lights from the Christmas tree glowed while RoseAnn strung another set. From the window, they could see her standing on a footstool to reach the top. She was humming a tune Sam recognized as "Silent Night." As she reached up to wrap the blinking chain through the branches, a white, longhaired cat came running toward her and lifted its paw at the dangling wire. A shape darted out of nowhere, and a loud bang sounded as a gun sent its bullet into the woman's back and she and the tree toppled backward toward the cat.

"No," Montmart screamed as he pulled the door open and pointed his gun at the killer who stood in his direct line of fire.

Sam's hand was on the time travel disk, and she instinctively pressed the center button but not before she saw who the detective's gun was aimed at. Standing by the dead body was a woman in black. Jane Oldsfield.

CHAPTER FIFTEEN

"Not I, not I, but the wind that blows through me! A fine wind is blowing the new direction of time."

— DAVID HERBERT LAWRENCE (1885-1930): "SONG OF A MAN WHO HAS COME THROUGH" (1920)

The digital pendulum clock beeped its fifth "chime." Sam and Montmart were back in Parsons' office. Montmart still had his finger on the trigger but was now pointing the gun at Parsons. When he realized he was no longer facing his wife's killer, he let it drop.

"It was hypnotism, wasn't it?" he asked.

Sam thought of the clock and, for a moment, she almost concurred with the detective. But then she realized he was only groping for the last explanation that would satisfy his doubt.

"No," Sam said softly, surprised to hear her own voice. "He's telling the truth, Philip. We were really back there. I know it's hard to believe, but this thing really works."

She walked across to Parsons and handed him the time-travel disk.

"Thanks, Sam."

"Why did Jane Oldsfield kill my wife?" Montmart asked, finally accepting what had been unacceptable to him thus far. "Neither one of us knew her."

"Are you sure of that? Could your wife have met her somewhere and not told you?"

Parsons replaced the disk in his desk drawer and locked it.

Montmart looked tired, as if the journey and/or its consequences had taken a toll on him. He sat on a chair next to the desk. "That's possible. RoseAnn was active in many associations. She also did a lot of volunteer work."

Sam took the seat next to him. Parsons was the only one standing. Then Sam saw why. His cat was curled up in his desk chair sound asleep after eating his lunch.

"If you knew that Jane killed RoseAnn because you've been back in Philip's past, don't you know why, too?"

"No. I've only seen selective parts of the past and that was before Jane took off with a dozen of the disks. The one you used is one of the two I have except for an additional microchip. I try not to use the disks because, if I get stuck in time, there'll be no one to stop her. That's why I need the two of you."

Sam was becoming annoyed at hearing bits and pieces of the story. "I think it's about time you told us everything, Greg. We didn't finish the notebook, but you can fill us in on the rest. What exactly do you want us to do?"

Parsons lifted Floppy from his chair and placed him on his lap. The cat repositioned himself and went back to sleep.

"You have to find the other time disks and destroy them or bring them back to me. She's messing with people's pasts, and we can't let her continue. If she succeeds and markets this product to the world, there's no telling the amount of damage that will occur." He petted Floppy's gray head and spoke in a low monotone as if crooning to the cat. "Jane likes to play games. I learned that too late, but at least it's helped me devise a plan. She gives hints at the end of her journal as to where she's hidden some of the disks. Those are the ones she's been able to anchor in time. She keeps the others on her."

"What about the cat?" Sam asked. "Jane said she implanted a microchip in him."

"Yes. I think she did that to get even with me. It would be too dangerous to remove that chip." He was still petting Floppy's head, and the cat was purring. "She sends him around in time and switches with him. She claims that's an easier way to transport. You see, until all the foundation disks are in place, the time you're allowed at a location once you transport is very limited. The chip Jane used on Floppy has a long transmittal time. It's too technical to explain. Let's just say, by switching with the cat, she can extend her time in the past or future from minutes to days and sometimes weeks at a time. That gives her the extra time she needs to find the correct locations to plant the disks."

Montmart looked even more stressed as he pulled out a cigarette and began smoking. "Hold on, Parsons. Are you telling us that Oldsfield travels through time to plant these disks in certain spots that will allow her to go back to that place and time whenever she wants?"

"That's a pretty accurate summation, Detective. It's a trial-and-error procedure, though, because she has to find exactly the right spots. I believe she's successfully planted two or three disks."

"If it's taking her so long and she's the one who created the disks, how can we be expected to find these locations?" Sam asked. "Wouldn't it be easier to get the disks off her?"

"If you can catch her. You probably have more of a chance of locating the disks she's planted."

"What about these clues you mentioned?" Montmart asked puffing a ring of smoke toward Parsons.

"They're in the book." He looked over at the desk where Sam had left the notebook before her journey back in time. "You can take it and finish reading it, but the hints or "clues" as you call them, are basically that she intends to plant five of the Foundation markers in the earth; four in the water; two in the air; and one in fire. Nine will be buried in the past; two in the future; and one in the present. I know she's already buried the present marker, but I don't know where. And, since the future markers can only be set up to twelve months ahead of time, I have a feeling she's working on those now. That's where I'd like you and Samantha to begin."

"When you say Oldsfield intends to bury the markers in certain elements, what does that mean?" Sam asked.

"The earth might be a farm, desert, or gardens – anywhere there's land. Water could be the ocean, a lake, or another body of water. Air is more nebulous and can be any area of high elevation; while fire can be in a volcano or a furnace."

"Sounds like some mystical nonsense," Montmart said. "How did she come up with all this?"

Parsons paused. "Jane is a brilliant woman. You could say she's ahead of her time. But very often people like her abuse their genius. After all, there's a thin line between genius and madness. When I met her at school, her aura of mystery intrigued me. I was attracted to her, and we started dating. She was actually just using me for my technical know-how. She needed me to complete this grand project she envisioned. At the time, she didn't realize the virtual travel program we'd created would ever be capable of time travel. When she discovered the power of our creation, she saw the profit potential while ignoring the ethical aspects I feared."

"Just a minute," Montmart stopped him, lighting up another cigarette. "Back up a bit. You said that you need us to find and destroy these time-travel disks. Even if we do that, won't Oldsfield just create more disks to plant? And what stops you from making more disks yourself?"

"The materials necessary to build the microchip for the disks currently exist only in minute quantities, but Jane is trying to find a way to mass produce them. She already mentioned to me, when she discovered the disks' time-travel potential that she intended to stop a proposal to ban the production of a radioactive compound that's one of the main components of the disks. She wanted to find a way to keep the compound in production so that the disks could be created and distributed worldwide. I'm afraid she may have found a way to do this, although she hasn't shared this information with me for the obvious reasons. You have no idea of the potential dangers this can create. If the disks fall into the wrong hands, people will be able to change time to their advantage."

"What's wrong with that?" Montmart asked raising a gray eyebrow. "If I could go back again, I'd save my wife. She was only twenty-nine when she died. We never had children. I was too much in a rush to even kiss her before I left the day she was killed. Hell, I would change time to my advantage. I'd take care of that bastard Oldsfield, and I wouldn't need a time disk to do it."

"That's exactly what I mean," Parsons said. "Do you think you're the only man who's lost his wife or his money or anything else of importance? Things happen because they're meant to happen. If we change time to suit ourselves, we're messing with destiny."

Sam thought of Angie and the family she'd lost in a fire as a young child, the impact it had on her and what Angie would give to take it all back, prevent it from happening. Sam, herself, might want to change a few things in her life. If she could go back, she'd never have started the ill-fated relationship with Peter and save herself the pain of the breakup but that was chicken soup compared to other people's problems and tragedies. Suddenly, Sam had another thought which she voiced aloud, "Wait a second, Greg, didn't you say that Jane mentioned to you that she was trying to stop a bill from passing that would ban the production of one of the time-travel disks' components?"

Parsons nodded.

"When did she say this?"

"I don't remember exactly. It was probably some time in December. Why?"

"Oh, my God!" Montmart exclaimed coming to the same conclusion as Sam. "Oldsfield murdered my wife because of the Rayore Bill. RoseAnn was petitioning with a group of environmentalists that supported it. She was working on an appeal to the president that she thought would have the bill passed."

"That's it," Parsons agreed. "That must be the reason. If Jane traveled to the future, she probably saw that the bill went through after the president received the letter and decided to kill the woman who'd written it." Floppy was beginning to stir on his lap. Greg turned to adjust his position, and the cat snuggled back to sleep.

"So, when do we begin our journeys?" Montmart asked, angry enthusiasm fueling his words.

"I have to teach you some lessons on how to use the disk. There are precautions you need to take. Since you won't have the cat to switch with like she does, you risk a phenomenon known as "parallel linkage." It happened to me once, and it wasn't a pleasant experience. Instead of transporting to one place and time, you end up being sent to multiple destinations and time periods. Eventually, you return to your starting point, but it's very disorienting."

"What if we use the cat to switch?" Sam asked.

As if responding to her question, Floppy chose that moment to jump off Parsons' lap and slide between Sam and Montmart's chairs. Sam reached down to pet him and was rewarded with a throaty purr.

"That's not possible. She saw to that. She has the controller device for his chip, and she'll use it again soon. I'm just glad Floppy hasn't gone back to any time periods in which cats weren't in favor, such as during the witch trials. Cats are well trained in self-preservation, unlike us humans, but he's been lucky so far that his instincts haven't been tested yet, at least I don't believe they have."

Sam had another idea. "What about my cat? Could you implant the microchip you have in her to switch?"

"You don't want to do that, Sam, do you?"

"How dangerous would it be to Holly?"

"There wouldn't be much danger involved in implanting it, only from the sedative I'd have to use to anesthetize her. The removal, on the other hand, would be tricky."

Montmart interrupted. "Forget the cat. Send us back again or forward in time. I think Sam needs further proof of your story before she lets you experiment on her pet."

Parsons nodded and opened his desk drawer to retrieve the time disk a second time. "I agree, although you risk parallel linkage." He walked over to them and held the disk out toward Sam. "Do you see the small silver numbers around the disk's outer edge?"

Sam squinted to read the tiny numerals that ran in a symmetrical pattern around the disk from the outer edge inward. "Yes. They seem to count repeatedly to thirty until they end at thirty in the center."

Parsons let Sam watch and Montmart, who'd stretched his head forward, as Greg moved one of the red arrow indicators clockwise around the circle three times. Sam was reminded of setting a light timer such as she'd set when she went away on vacation. She'd always had a tough time with those and knew this would be even harder to manipulate.

"When I turn the dial clockwise, I'm setting the travel for the future. Likewise, if I turn it counterclockwise, I'd be setting it for past transport. Since I circled the disk three times around thirty, which represents days in the future but years in the past, you would be headed approximately three months forward in time. Got that so far?"

Sam nodded, but Montmart seemed stymied. "If that's the time setting, how do you set the place?"

"That's a bit more complicated. It's done by computer code for various regions." Parsons turned the disk over and showed the detective some buttons on the back. "I press a series of numbers for time zones, latitudes, and longitudes and that's where you go, give or take any discrepancy in the geographic range of the transport."

Montmart looked unimpressed. "Cut the techno crap and just tell us where you're sending us."

"Not far, actually. You'll be headed to Manhattan about three months from now." He gave Sam back the disk, gently opening her fingers to close around it. "Don't forget the center button to come back if it gets too overwhelming, but it won't work in parallel linkage. You'll get back, though, don't worry about that." He turned toward the detective who stood up as Sam rose. "Put your hand on top of hers as before and apply a bit of light pressure. I'll see you both here in around three seconds my time, fifteen or twenty minutes, yours."

CHAPTER SIXTEEN

"Time is an illusion."

— ALBERT EINSTEIN

The clock wasn't chiming this time, but Sam almost heard its mechanical rings in her mind. Montmart's hand was warm and moist in hers. Although he seemed calm, she knew he was as nervous as she was. A strange thought ran through her mind before she realized she was no longer in Parsons' office. She wondered if it got any easier the more times you did it, like an actor performing on stage or a trapeze artist preparing for a high dive. This feeling was caused by the same rush of adrenaline but without the eyes of the audience upon you.

"Do you know where we are?" Montmart asked.

Sam looked around at the snow-covered street and the Christmas lights that blazed warmly from windows into the cold night into which she and the detective had descended. For a moment, she feared they were back at Montmart's house before his wife's murder, reenacting the scene once more. Then she realized that they were neither by the Old Brookville house, nor were they in Manhattan. Instead, Sam recognized her old

Hicksville neighborhood. They were on a block not far from her mother's house.

"We're on Long Island. In Hicksville," Sam said. "It seems to be December or maybe early January. Parsons said three months, but I think the transport was off. At least it was for the location."

"Let's hope we don't experience that parallel linkage thing," Montmart said. "What are we supposed to do now?"

"I don't know about you, but I'd like to get out of the cold." Sam shivered as a gust of wind blew in her direction. Without a coat, the freezing temperature bit into her like a hungry wolf ravishing a juicy steak. She rubbed her ungloved hands and found she still held the time-travel disk.

Montmart didn't seem to mind the cold, although his cheeks were turning red except the area where the white scar made a broad contrast. "Looks like there's a restaurant or a place to eat down there." He glanced toward the end of the block. Sam recognized the neighborhood bar her sister liked to frequent. She'd only been there once with Jennifer and couldn't even recall its name. She followed the detective, trudging through a snowbank, toward the glowing oasis. The seedy little building was on a corner next to a seedier house that had no Christmas decorations and appeared to be vacant or occupied by renters who used it as a dwelling and not a home. The bar was Charlie's, but the only red bulbs left on its marquee spelt "Char ... s."

As they walked through the door, loud rock music from ceiling speakers blasted through them like the last gust of wind as they blew inside. Sam's cold ears revolted against the noise. If they were numb, she only imagined what the full octave range sounded like. Jennifer liked her music loud with incomprehensible lyrics.

"Isn't that your sister?" Montmart asked, raising his voice so she could hear.

Sam looked in the direction he was staring. Jennifer sat on a barstool next to a guy with long brown hair. They were laughing and drinking alternately, unable to hold a conversation above the noise and not really wanting to. *No wonder a bar is such a good place for meaningless relationships,* Sam thought.

Just as Sam considered approaching her sister, Jennifer swaggered off the barstool, gave the longhaired guy a quick kiss on the lips, and started for the door. Montmart pushed Sam out of the way as Jennifer walked toward them.

"What are you doing?"

"She can't see us. We're not supposed to be here."

Sam had forgotten they were in the future. As she and the detective huddled in the corner near the men's room door which looked as if it had knife gauges in it, Jennifer left the bar.

"She's probably headed home," Sam said. "I have no idea what time it is, but she likes to stay out late. Mom is waiting for her. She always does but says it's because she can't sleep with all her aches and pains. She used to wait up for me, too, but I'd get the lectures. Jen can stay out all night, and Mom will welcome her home with open arms."

"Maybe that's because she's still there," Montmart said. "Your mom's alone in that house now, isn't she, except for your sister?"

Sam knew that was true, but she didn't reply. For some reason, the detective's unasked for deduction bothered her.

"Let's follow her," Sam said, changing the subject.

"You're sure you want to go back out in the cold?"

"My house is nearby. If Parsons is right, we should be back in his office in about five minutes, anyway."

Montmart didn't look like a happy camper, and she realized he'd been as affected by the cold as she'd been but hadn't wanted to admit it. His stoic façade annoyed her.

When Sam and Montmart left Charlie's, heading in the direction Sam indicated, they saw Jennifer's red Camaro tear around the corner and then heard a mind-wrenching screech. Ignoring the cold, Sam ran through the snow, nearly falling several times on black ice, until she arrived at the scene of what was a serious accident.

The car was smashed up against a light post that Jennifer must've hit in her drunken daze. At the speed she was traveling, the impact had been horrific.

"Oh, my God!" Sam cried as people on the street and in nearby houses ran to help.

As she tried to make her way to the car, Montmart put his arm out to stop her just as she'd done when he'd tried to enter his house during his wife's murder. "Don't, Sam. You shouldn't see this. Give me the disk. We should go back."

Sam wasn't listening. She watched as a police car with its red blinking lights pulled up and two officers started clearing people away. One of them pulled Jennifer's body from the car. She saw him lift up her limp hand and check for a pulse and then shake his head at his fellow officer.

"No," Sam screamed.

Montmart held her back. "Give me the disk, Sam."

All of a sudden, the world went black. Sam thought she'd fainted but found herself outside what appeared to be a farmhouse. It was a bright blue day with barely a cloud in the sky, and the temperature was mild and pleasant. *Where am I?* she thought, *"and where's Jennifer?"* Then she recalled Parsons' warning about the parallel linkage transporting her to different times. She looked around for Montmart, but the detective wasn't there. She still held the time disk in her hand. For a moment, she wanted to press the center emergency button but recalled that Parsons said that wouldn't work in parallel linkage.

She stood a few feet from the farmhouse's door in a field of wildflowers. She thought about the photo she'd seen of Montmart's wife, but the small house before her looked nothing like the home in Brookville. As she wandered through the buttercups and clover toward the rustic structure, she heard a cat crying in the distance. An orange tabby came out from behind a wheelbarrow by the side of the house, and Sam was startled to see that it was her cat, Holly.

As she was about to call to the cat, the farmhouse's door

opened and a voice, like an eerie echo, sent a chill up her spine. Holly, responding to her name, ran to the door. The woman framed in the doorway wasn't looking her way, but Sam saw her clearly from where she stood. In an old pair of jeans and one of her favorite sweaters, Sam came face to face with herself.

The future Sam picked Holly up as she came in the house and gave her a hug. A man called out from behind her and then came to put his arms around the pair. Sam was shocked to see Greg Parsons embracing her future self and her cat. The couple looked so happy and in love.

Sam felt like a witness to her own fate as she watched the two kiss. She turned away in embarrassment and found herself in a white hospital corridor. Parsons had been right about the disorientation of the parallel linkage. She just wished her time in the future were up so that she could return to the present.

Nurses and orderlies scurried down the halls like actors and actresses on ER. Sam avoided a near collision with a grufflooking nurse carrying a clipboard. "What are you doing in here, Miss?" she asked. "If you're visiting someone in the Maternity Ward, I need to see your pass. Visiting hours are nearly over."

Maternity ward? Sam had no idea why she was in that part of the hospital, or even what hospital she was in. "I'm sorry. I must've gotten lost," she muttered. "Where is the waiting room?"

The nurse pointed down the corridor to the right. In a loud whisper she exclaimed to a younger nurse who was passing by, "That one was trying to sneak in. I hope it's not another one like we had last week trying to steal a baby."

As Sam attempted to make her way to the waiting room hoping she would be linked back to her own time soon, she passed one of the patient's rooms and couldn't help but overhear pitiful sobbing.

A man's soothing voice was trying to console his wife or girlfriend. "It's going to be okay, Angie."

Now Sam's attention was hooked. It couldn't be. She paused

outside the door and bent forward to peer into the darkened room. She recognized her friend immediately even though her face was red and swollen with tear streaks.

"It isn't going to be okay, Mark," Angie cried. "our baby is deformed. He's a freak, and it's all my fault. I must've done something wrong, and now he's going to pay for it the rest of his life."

The words cut through Sam's mind like a knife. She wanted to run in the room and comfort her friend. Preoccupied with the drama, Sam didn't hear someone come up behind her until she felt a tap on her shoulder. Jumping around quickly in surprise, she faced the suspicious nurse.

"If you don't leave this ward soon, Miss, I'm afraid I'm going to have to call security."

"I'm leaving. I just need to find my way out of here," Sam said truthfully.

That was the last thing she remembered before she found herself looking, not at the sourpuss-faced nurse but into the dark blue eyes of Greg Parsons.

She flushed with embarrassment as she recalled the love scene she'd witnessed on the previous time journey. She hoped he mistook her reddened face for the exertion of the transport.

"Where's Montmart?" he asked, ignoring her completely.

"Oh, no. Is he stuck in the future?"

Parsons nodded. "I'm afraid so. He must've broken the link which means that he won't be able to get back here without help from us."

"The last time he was with me we were by anaccident, my sister's car crash." The memory of the future vision caused Sam to shudder. "You said we can't change the past, but is there any way we can change the future? If I could warn Jennifer or prevent her from driving or going to that bar ..."

Parsons waved his hand as if dismissing her. "You have to realize that where you've been may never happen. The present is changing the future constantly. What you've seen is just one possible future."

"Is that where Montmart is? Still at the scene of the accident?"

"No. I believe he may have linked into his own future. Did you travel anywhere else?

Sam thought of the cottage in the country and blushed again. "Yes. There were two other places."

"You parallel linked. I was afraid of that." Parsons approached her, and she feared he noticed her redness. "You're going to have to go back, or should I say, forward again and try to reestablish the link so that you can bring back the detective."

Sam was listening with one part of her mind and wondering with the other if this man had actually seen his own future with her as she had seen it with him. "How do I do that?" she asked in a voice that sounded like a little girl's.

Parsons placed his hand in hers, and for a moment, she didn't realize what he was doing, but he was only reaching for the time-travel disk. "I'll need to go with you, as dangerous as that is. A triple transport back will be extremely risky, but we have to give it a shot. The important thing is not to let go of my hand. By repeating the transport, we could end up back in your future or, hopefully, in Montmart's."

"Wait a minute," Sam said pulling his hand and the disk away. "Before I go anywhere again, I need to know what type of danger you're talking about. Could I end up stuck in time, too?"

Parsons didn't have to answer. His expression told her she'd made the correct assumption.

"Isn't there an alternative?"

"Switching's the only other way. Jane's sent Floppy back, though. I knew she would."

Sam hadn't even noticed the cat missing. "What about my cat? I offered her earlier, and you said it could be done."

He paused. "We'd have to do it right away. The longer we wait, the less chance we have of transporting to the right coordinates and locating Montmart. If I go back with you to the city, that will save some time. The procedure doesn't take long." He was talking himself into it, scouring his desk for the equipment he needed. Sam saw him reach into another drawer and take out a small, gray bag that looked like an oversized wallet.

"Everything I need is here. Are you ready?"

CHAPTER SEVENTEEN

"Time Present and Time Past are both perhaps present in Time Future, and Time Future contained in Time Past."

— THOMAS STEARNS ELIOT "FOUR QUARTERS, BURNT NORTON" [1935]

S am felt a sense of foreboding, yet at the same time a strange inner calm, as she walked besides Parsons out of Virtual Software's building. On the way from the elevator to the exit, Parsons greeted a few people who were either going to or returning from lunch. He acknowledged them briefly with a smile and a hello but didn't introduce Sam nor initiate any further conversation.

It was drizzling outdoors, but Sam could care less about the weather. Spotting Montmart's car in the parking lot, a fresh pang of guilt hit her. Why had she agreed to participate in the time-travel demonstration, and why had Parsons sent her and the detective forward at such a risk? Now she was even going to sacrifice her cat.

Parsons, sensing her misgivings, took her gently by the arm and said, "Don't worry, Sam. Everything's going to be okay. I'll be with you this time, and I know the system inside and out. As long as we use Holly as a grounder, we'll be fine."

Sam wasn't relieved, but the light pressure of the man's touch made her feel a bit better. When they got to his car, a maroon Mazda, Greg opened the passenger door and let her in. She was reminded of Montmart's lack of manners, which hadn't distracted from his natural charm. Parsons, on the other hand, performed his gentlemanly duties stiffly, almost mechanically. She didn't find much charm in that and wondered how much of his behavior was rehearsed. She still couldn't trust this man and recalled Montmart's warnings that Parsons and Oldsfield might be involved in illegal doings.

As Greg got behind the wheel, squeezing his large frame into the small car, he looked over at her. "I know you don't fully believe everything I've told you," he said as if reading her mind, "and I thank you for going along with me this far. I'm sorry about the detective. Parallel linkage is a rare phenomenon." He paused. "I realize that witnessing your sister's car accident must've been awful, but there's no guarantee it'll ever occur. I hope the other linkages weren't as negative for you."

Sam heard the question in his voice and wondered if he knew about her vision of their romantic rendezvous. She turned to the rain-sprinkled window, away from his deep blue eyes. "I also witnessed the birth of my best friend's baby. I didn't see it, but she was crying that it was deformed. She and her fiancée are getting married in two months, and I'm in the wedding party."

"That's too bad, but I wouldn't tell her. Like I said, it may never happen."

She turned to face him. "What if it does? Angie has had so many tough breaks in her life. This would destroy her."

"Calm down, Sam. The future isn't solid like the past. It's a shifting liquid that can change shape at any time."

"Then why did I see those things? If I actually went forward in time ..." She kept quiet about the love scene between them she'd seen in the second linkage.

It was Greg who turned away this time to start the car. "I can't explain it to you right now. We have to get into the city and work on your cat before Montmart does anything foolish in any of his linkages."

"You mean try to stop his wife's murder? What if he does save his wife? What would happen?"

"You don't want to know." Parsons pulled out of the parking lot. He switched his windshield wipers on low to wipe away the spotty rain. "The consequences are very bad."

"I really can't understand any of this." Sam spoke her thoughts aloud.

"You don't have to. Just trust me."

Said the spider to the fly …

Their eyes met for a moment, and Sam felt a strange connection. It was as though she had no choice but to trust him against her better judgment, as though fate had already decreed her decision.

When they arrived at Sam's apartment, the light rain had turned into a downpour. Sam rushed into the stairway foyer with Greg at her dripping heels. She almost slipped on the parquet floor tiles into his arms and wondered briefly if that would also have been ordained by fate. She'd never thought so much about the past and the future in her whole life as she'd done in the last three days.

The door to her apartment was open with Angie standing there watching her ascend the stairs. "It's about time, Missy," her friend said without a touch of annoyance.

Yes, Sam thought, *it is about time. Time is exactly what it's about.* She stepped into her living room, and Holly came racing toward her making her feel even guiltier. She reached down and rubbed the little red head. "Thanks for cat sitting, Angie." She turned back toward Parsons. "You remember Greg Parsons from Virtual Software."

Angie looked Parsons over with the eye of a photographer. "Nice to see you again. I don't know if I told you the first time we met that you're even sexier than your web page photo."

Sam didn't give Greg the opportunity to respond. "This is my friend, Angie, the girl who got me the interview with you under false pretenses. She's the one who's getting married in two months."

"Seven weeks."

"In a rush, are we?" Parsons grinned. "I'm sorry to be rude, but Sam and I have something important to attend to that requires prompt action. Maybe we can chat another time."

Sam realized Parsons' mistake before Angie replied to his inferred request for her to leave. She knew her friend was perpetually curious and couldn't be put off that easily.

"What's going on?" Angie asked turning to Sam. "You two appear out of the blue and rush me away like you're hiding something." Then, as if she'd thought about her words after she'd spoken them, she raised a blonde brow and added, "Oh, now I've figured it out. Excuse me, I'll leave you two alone to your, uh, urgent project."

Sam could've laughed at the expression on her friend's face and her exaggerated emphasis on the word "project." Angie thought Sam and Greg were asking her to leave so they could be alone for a romantic encounter. If she knew the truth, she'd be surprised and a lot less safe. *Ignorance was bliss and often safer than knowledge,* Sam reflected.

When Angie was gone, with a goodbye kiss for Holly and Sam and a wave to Greg, Sam asked, "What do you need me to do?"

"Try to relax the cat as much as possible. Hold her in your lap. As soon as I give her the sedative, she'll be asleep."

Sam picked up Holly and carried her to the couch. The cat already instinctively knew something was up as she wriggled in her owner's arms.

"Please, Holly, you're going to be okay," Sam said trying to console herself as well as her pet.

When Holly settled down, Parsons sat next to Sam and petted the cat, talking to her soothingly as he reached into his bag and extracted the sedative. "Floppy always hated needles," he explained as he injected Holly. "The trick is to pretend that nothing special is happening." Within minutes, Holly closed her eyes and was asleep on Sam's lap.

"What now?"

"I need more light and a stable surface. I'll move her into the kitchen to the table. You don't have to watch."

"I'll watch. I'm not afraid of blood."

"She won't bleed much, and there won't be anything too upsetting to see. I just thought you'd rather wait here. It doesn't take long."

Sam didn't know whether Greg preferred to do the procedure unwatched, or he was warning her that there was a likelihood something might go wrong. "That's okay. I'd rather be with her." Sam picked up Holly and carried her into the kitchen. She felt heavy and warm. She didn't stir, even when Sam laid her down on the table.

Parsons took some tiny tools and a microchip out of his bag and laid them in a neat row next to the cat. The procedure took less than fifteen minutes as he shaved a bit of fur from around the tuft of the neck where Holly's mother must've carried her around as a kitten and made a tiny incision into which he inserted the disk. Sam thought of chips used to identify cats and wanted to ask him if this was the same procedure but didn't want to interrupt his concentration.

After he'd sutured two tiny stitches to hold the wound shut, he turned to her and smiled. "That should do it. I gave her a light sedative, so she should be awake in about fifteen minutes or so. You can put her back on the couch. Just hold her gently and watch her neck."

"When will we be able to travel?"

"As soon as she's up and about. I could transport her now, but that would be too risky with her still under the sedative. Once she's transported, we don't have to wait at all."

"What if he's already changed time?" Sam knew Greg would understand that she was referring to Montmart and whether he'd found his wife and prevented her murder.

"There still might be something we can do. I'd rather we didn't have to, though. Tampering with time is dangerous."

Sam took Holly gently in her arms. "Will she be in any pain when she awakens?"

"No. She might feel fuzzy from the sedative, that's all."

"I hope we find him in time."

"So do I."

CHAPTER EIGHTEEN

"Men talk of killing time, while time quietly kills them."

— DION BOUCICAULT

While they waited for Holly's sedative to wear off, Sam made them each a cup of coffee. Greg's eyes remained glued to the cat and her softly rising stomach as she slumbered peacefully.

"She looks like a kitten sleeping like that," he said taking the coffee mug Sam passed him.

"Like a little angel until she starts tearing paper to shreds when I don't give her enough attention. Angie got so mad once when Holly tore up one of her photos."

"Maybe she needs a brother or sister. Have you ever considered adopting another cat?"

"I have, and I still may. It's just that I don't have time to spend housebreaking and raising a new kitten."

"It doesn't have to be a kitten." Greg poured a touch of milk into his coffee. "There are lots of older cats in need of homes."

"That could be worse. An older cat is harder to train because it's set in its ways." Sam was tiring of the conversation that she felt was only Greg's way of marking time. He must've realized it because he didn't pursue the topic.

After a few minutes of sitting in silence with only the low stirrings of Holly's breaths to interrupt their thoughts, Parsons returned to a more pertinent subject. "I'm sorry I got you involved in this, Sam, but I didn't have much of a choice."

"I thought you said the future can change. Why are you so sure I'm the one who can stop Jane?"

He set down his almost full mug. He'd only had a few sips, while Sam was ready for another cup. "It's hard to explain, and I have to admit I could be wrong. If I am, I apologize to you as well as to myself and likely to the whole world. The only justification I can give isn't based on any of the science I studied with Jane. It's a gut feeling, Sam, and I don't get gut feelings too often. Well, maybe I do, but I'm so used to ignoring them. I guess I'm like an adult who's forgotten how to act like a kid. Does any of that make sense?"

Sam placed her empty cup next to his. "Actually, it does, Greg." She hardly noticed her adaption of his first name, but she was sure he had. She continued, "When I met you, you seemed like a scientific know-it-all. But there were contradictions in your personality that I couldn't explain."

"Such as?"

"Well, there was the fact that you'd worked as a journalist before becoming a computer programmer. Then there's the tan."

"The tan?" Greg looked down at his dark forearms. "That's from golf. I took the sport up two years ago. It helps me relax and get outdoors away from those metal boxes. I also have a house in the country away from the maddening crowd. As for the writing, I wrote for technical journals. That's a far cry from being an emotional novelist."

"Perhaps, but it still shows a hidden depth. You're an abstract painting. Most people are." Sam paused and pushed on besides her better judgment. "I don't know how well acquainted we've become in the future, but there are a lot of things I don't know about you now that I wish I did."

"Do one of those things concern my past relationship with Jane?"

Before Sam could reply, a meow announced Holly's awakening. The cat stretched and then turned around and settled back down into a sleepy orange ball of fur.

"She's up," Greg said. "She just doesn't want to face the world yet." He glanced at his watch. "However, she's going to have to. Maybe you should feed her or to get her going."

Sam dreaded this more than Greg's last question. "I guess that means we're on our way, too?"

"Hopefully." He stood up and took the time-travel disk out of his pants pocket. "I'm setting this for the closest coordinates to where we lost Montmart. He may no longer be there but remember that our time advances faster than his."

Sam moved closer to Holly and ran her palm gently through the cat's fur. "It's wake-up time, honey. I'll get you some dinner." She had to choke back a tear at the thought that she might never see her beloved pet again. If Greg's gut feeling was wrong and she was taking this risk for nothing ...

Holly came running, albeit a little slowly and less sprightly, when Sam opened her favorite can of cat food. She still seemed a bit fuzzyheaded and her eyes had a dull, glazed look from the drugs.

"Are you sure she's ready?" Sam asked Greg as he joined her in the kitchen.

"She'll be fine. It's us I'm worried about." He seemed about to say something else but shrugged off whatever was in his mind as he aimed the time disk at Holly.

"Wait!" Sam looked down at the cat. She could feel the tears behind her eyes. "Before you send her, maybe I should put on her collar. She only wears it when I take her to the vet, but at least it'll be some identification."

Greg smiled. "You're like a worried mother fussing over that cat. Floppy's been traveling back and forth in time for months without tags. The microchip is all we need to keep her in range and that won't get caught on trees."

"I guess you're right." Sam sighed, then reached down and gave Holly a final pet. "Take care, Sweetie."

Without further ado, Greg pressed the button on the disk. Holly was gone in a second, only the half-eaten cat food in the pet dish evidence she'd ever been there.

"Our turn, Sam. Take my hand."

"Are we joining Holly, or is she coming back here?"

"She'll be back safe on her cat tree or wherever else she likes to cozy. We'll be where Montmart was sent when the parallel linkage split the two of you up."

Sam shivered. "Maybe we're the ones who need ID tags," she said with a weak laugh.

Greg didn't comment. Instead, he closed his warm hand over her cold one and pressed the time-travel disk. Sam felt that fluttery feeling she'd experienced each time she'd been transported. It felt like the exact moment a plane took off the ground, only the plane was her body. She closed her eyes and gulped. When she opened them, she found herself with Greg in the middle of chaos.

They were standing outside Montmart's house. The door was wide open to the scene inside that resembled a nightmarish Christmas Carol. Jane Oldsfield stood at the tree with the gun in her hand. In front of her lay Montmart face down in a pool of blood. From his position, it seemed he'd run into the house at the moment Jane had aimed the gun at his wife. RoseAnn wasn't there.

"Oh, my God!" Sam exclaimed. "She's killed him instead."

"Quiet, Sam. She's still got the gun, and she's after RoseAnn. We have to find her."

"What about Phillip?"

"We can't do anything about him now. Not yet."

"There's two of us. If we can get the gun away from her, we might be able to save him if he's still alive."

"That's too dangerous. I think she knows we're here."

As if revealing the truth to his words, Jane turned in the direction of the door and came toward them.

"Come with me. Hurry!" Greg pulled Sam's hand and led her around the side of the house. To keep up with him, she found her legs running but didn't realize she'd commanded them to do so. Her whole body seemed frozen but not from the cold.

Montmart's landscaped backyard was as lovely in winter as it had been in summer when she'd been there with him in the future. Evergreens adorned with Christmas lights flanked the exterior adding a shimmering, surreal feeling to this surreal experience. *Was this the way she would die? Holding the hand of a man who was fated to be her lover in a future that would never be.*

Sam heard the fast clicking of Jane's high heels on the graveled walk as she raced after them. She was thankful for her own low heels and the fact that she could keep up the pace with Greg who hadn't let a sedentary job stop him from keeping fit.

"We have to hide. We can't keep running." Greg grabbed her abruptly and pulled her into a bush by the back door. "We won't be able to stay here long," he whispered. "We might have to go into the house and try to get back out the front door."

"Why don't we just transport back to our time?" she asked in a responding whisper.

"We have to find RoseAnn. She may have gotten away. If she has, it's too late."

"What do you mean?"

Greg didn't have time to answer. They heard Jane rounding the corner. Sam took the initiative this time and pulled Greg toward the back door. Luckily, it was open. They slipped inside and found themselves in the sunroom which was covered over for the winter. The lounge and chair where Philip had cornered Floppy had white sheets draped over them like ghosts late for a Halloween party.

There were assorted Christmas decorations in boxes that were either ready for the tree or not going to be used this year. Sam nearly stumbled in the dark as she tried to avoid a tangle of light strings and bulbs that were lying on the floor around a few boxes.

"Be careful," Greg whispered. "Once you're in the main part of the house, head upstairs."

"Upstairs? Greg, do you really think RoseAnn would've gone there? She's probably trying to get away."

"Not necessarily. She might be trying to get back to Montmart to see if he's alive – or she could be trying to get to a phone to call the police."

"If RoseAnn's upstairs, why is Jane pursuing us?"

"Because we have the time-travel disk. Please, Sam, I don't have time to explain. Let's just go."

The sunroom door creaked as Jane entered. Sam heeded Greg's words and fled toward the French doors that opened into the foyer leading to the living room.

They were on the second landing when they heard Jane's voice, "Stop right there. You're both fools. You can't save her."

Greg ignored Jane and continued pulling Sam up the stairs behind him. Suddenly, like the ghost that she actually was, RoseAnn appeared. Greg nearly collided with her as he reached the second floor. She was hysterical. Between sobs and jittery movements, Sam could just make out that RoseAnn had discovered all the phone lines in the house cut and that she knew downstairs was her only venue of escape.

"Can any of the windows upstairs open?" Greg asked, not stopping to introduce himself or Sam because introductions weren't possible at the moment.

"I didn't try them," RoseAnn sobbed. "But, Philip, is he, is he?" Her question trailed off in a wail.

Greg took the hysterical woman's arm and guided her back up the way she'd come. In doing so, he had to let go of Sam's hand. "Here, take the disk," he said turning back to Sam briefly. "Guard it with your life and stay close."

Acknowledging the fact that Greg had ignored her command, Jane pursued them, her high heels beating a deadly staccato up the wooden steps.

Greg led RoseAnn into the master bedroom at the end of the hall. Sam followed them into a room that was far removed from the one in which she'd spent the night less than a day ago. The bare, masculine tones were gone and in their place were soft, feminine touches – lace, eyelet curtains on the windows; an array of incandescent perfume bottles, candles, and potpourri holders on the nightstand to the right of the bed that must've been Rose-Ann's side, and a fluffy white Persian cat that at first glance seemed to be stuffed. Sam thought it odd that the animal had remained at the foot of the bed while chaos was erupting through the house. Before she could think of a reason why, Jane bounded into the room, her dark clothes and black gun making an eerie contrast to the bright room.

"Give me the disk, Greg, and I'll let you all go free," she said.

"Do you think I'm crazy? Maybe I was once when I let you charm me, but I know better now." He looked over at me. "Sam, take my hand and press the button."

"Don't listen to him," Jane said, pointing the gun at RoseAnn. Sam heard the click of the gun's catch. The cat rushed off its comfortable spot on the bed and made a mad dash for the door. "Greg pushed Roseann toward Sam and stepped in front of the two women. For a deadly second, there was nothing between Greg and the trigger of Jane's gun. Sam knew it was now or never. She grabbed RoseAnn's hand and pressed it around the disk. She could feel the cold trembling of the woman's fingers as they clung to hers. "Please, RoseAnn, take Greg's hand. We can get away, but we have to stick together." In her blind fear, RoseAnn wasn't in a position to question the foolhardiness of such an act. She had no way of knowing Sam held the means of their escape between their shaking palms.

RoseAnn reached out tentatively toward Greg who was

inching his way back toward them. But before he could grasp RoseAnn's outstretched hand, Jane fired.

"Sorry, Greg, but I think I gave you enough warning."

Sam gasped. Greg lay on the floor. She didn't know exactly where he'd been shot, only that it had been at point-blank range. She was in too much shock to realize that RoseAnn had knelt down beside him and taken his hand. Neither did she know whether she'd pressed the time travel disk or had merely squeezed her fingers into a fist around it. All she knew was that she, RoseAnn, and Greg were suddenly back in her apartment with Holly licking Greg's face to revive him.

Thankfully, the bullet wound was in Greg's shoulder. He came to in surprise more than pain and sat up abruptly as he wiped his face free of Holly's ministerings. "Ugh, cat saliva!"

Sam sat down next to him. "We have to get you to a hospital. That looks pretty bad."

Greg glanced at his left shoulder and winced as he realized he'd been shot. "It looks worse than it feels unless I'm still in shock. The blood's making me queasy, though."

"I might be able to help," RoseAnn said. "I'm a nurse." Her voice sounded steady, but Sam wondered what she was thinking of her first time-travel experience.

"Thanks, but there isn't time," Greg told her. "Jane will be right on our heels. I suppose you need an explanation for all this, but I'll have to make it quick. By time traveling, Jane discovered that you would be instrumental in passing a bill that outlaws a hazardous environmental compound needed to produce the time-travel disks she plans to market and sell in the present time. To assure that this compound remains in production, she killed you before the bill went through. Now it's up to Sam and me to prevent her from going through with her plans. Your husband got involved and became more interested in saving your life. In trying to do that, he lost his. The only solution is to go back again before Jane shoots him and changes the past. Do you understand?"

RoseAnn proved a lot more accepting of the incredible than her husband, possibly because she'd just experienced it first-hand. "Yes. It means I have to die. The compound you referred to is Rayore. The legislation is up for the end of the year. I have a campaign party scheduled for tomorrow night."

"Isn't there any other way?" Sam asked. "What if we bring Philip and RoseAnn forward to our time? If RoseAnn lives and the bill passes, won't Jane be forced to abandon her project?"

"I wish it were that simple." Greg reached out and petted Holly's head that was nuzzling against his unwounded shoulder. "Although the future can change, the past can't. RoseAnn died, and the Rayore bill was defeated."

"These time travel rules confuse me." Sam walked over to RoseAnn. "I'm sorry. Greg's right. Philip has to live, and you have to die."

"I'd rather it be me, anyway."

"Give me the time-travel disk," Greg said after the three considered RoseAnn's words.

Sam handed him the disk. He set the coordinates and handed it back to her. "I'm in no condition to accompany you. Besides, I know you can handle this."

"Will you be okay?" He was beginning to look very pale. Sam didn't know whether it was from the loss of blood or his fear for their safety.

"If you go back and do it right, I should be as fit as ever."

Sam smiled at his attempt at a joke. She went over to him and kissed him gently on the cheek. "If anything goes wrong, call an ambulance. Make sure Angie adopts Holly. I'd want her to have a good home."

CHAPTER NINETEEN

"And thus the whirligig of time brings in his revenges."

— SHAKESPEARE "TWELFTH NIGHT"

The coordinates Greg set were perfectly aligned to the time at which Sam and RoseAnn needed to arrive. Philip stood in the door's entryway ready to spring. It seemed like a slow-motion picture to Sam who watched Jane aim the gun at the minutes younger RoseAnn as she innocently wrapped garland around a glittering tree. The other RoseAnn was at Sam's side taking in the scene with a mix of awe and fear.

Just as Philip placed his hand on the door to pull it open, RoseAnn rushed past Sam. "No, Phil. Please, don't do it. I'm meant to die. You're meant to live. She has to kill me."

Montmart whirled around in surprise. "My God, RoseAnn!"

Sam fought an impulse to back away and leave the two of them to their last moments together. Only the time-travel disk in her hand and the knowledge she had to transport Montmart back with her as soon as time had corrected itself, kept her glued to the side of the parting lovers. Nonetheless, it was as if she wasn't there as far as they were concerned.

"I have to stop her, Rosie. You're too young to die. I need you with me. I can't live without you." There were tears in Philip's eyes, and Sam felt her eyes also water with the emotion of the scene.

"Yes, you can, Phil. I want you to. You'll meet someone else one day. Just remember that I love you, and I want you to have a happy life. Don't disappoint me, and promise me you'll take good care of Lulu."

"I don't think I can keep those promises. I could never replace you, and seeing Lulu will just remind me of losing you. But I promise I'll find a good home for her."

Suddenly, there was the sound of a gun's backfire. Sam and Philip turned their attention to the living room and saw RoseAnn lying dead under the tree. "No," Montmart cried turning back to the future RoseAnn who was no longer there. Sam acted quickly. She grabbed Philip's hand and pressed the button of the time-travel disk to transport them forward to their current time.

"Welcome back," Greg said to the two time travelers from his spot on Sam's couch where he was scratching behind Holly's ears. The cat purred loudly. Sam was glad to see Greg's injured arm no longer contained a bullet hole.

Sam still held Philip's hand. "Are you okay?" she asked him.

"I will be. I have to admit I don't understand a lot about this time-travel business. And I thought it was a ruse when I first heard about it. But now … Well, I wanted to save her. I should feel terrible that I didn't. But I understand in a way. And I feel relieved." He grinned, "Damn it, I don't even feel like smoking. At least I got a chance to say goodbye."

"That's more than some of us get," Greg said, rising from the couch. "But it's not over yet. If you're with me now, Phil, the three of us can work together to stop Jane. I have a plan. It involves traveling back to the time Rayore was created in a lab in

Utah. I think Jane might've gone back there and hidden one of the disks. It makes sense for her to start at the beginning. Are both of you willing to join me?"

Montmart smiled. "Why the hell not? I've always wanted justice to be done, but I realize now I can't change time to do it. The most important thing in my life was RoseAnn, and I lost her. The second most important thing was to even the score with her killer. I'll do anything, go anywhere, to do that."

"Just remember that RoseAnn wants you to go on living," Sam said. "Don't try anything risky this time."

Greg took Sam's free hand. "We all have to keep an eye on one another. Give me the disk, Sam, I'll set it for Orem, Utah, October 1993."

The farthest West Sam had ever traveled was to Chicago for a library conference nearly ten years ago. But when she considered the time traveling that she'd done recently, Orem, Utah, seemed as close as Long Island was to Manhattan. Orem was the headquarters for WordPerfect, the software company that had taken the nation by storm not too long ago to eventually fall behind to mighty Microsoft's Word program.

As soon as Sam transported there with Greg and Philip at her side, she marveled at the round edifice of Piefenberg Labs set back in a mountain. The desert was warm but not sweltering on this October day five years past. The sky was overcast, and the sand, like autumn leaves, swirled in eddies around their legs.

"This is it," Greg said. "Piefenberg is where Rayore was born. Jane used to tell me the story like a fairytale a mother tells a child."

"Doesn't look like much," Philip added. "No wonder RoseAnn wasn't impressed. All those people dumping chemicals in the desert. Sometimes you wonder if technology is the devil's gift."

"Technology offers society essential benefits if used in the proper way." Greg was touchy on this subject because technology was his life. Sam's views laid somewhere between theirs. "What do we do now?" She just wanted to get the job done and return to her own time and place.

"We wait, watch, and listen."

"Bullshit!" Montmart wasn't a patient man. "I thought you said we were coming back to destroy that hidden disk you think Jane planted here somewhere. If that's the case, we should be searching for it not digging our feet in the sand." He grinned when he realized the pun he'd made.

"We'd save more time observing what's going on in the lab. If the disk hasn't been hidden yet, we could catch Jane in the act. If she's already hidden it, we could pick up some clues."

"Parsons, I'm the detective here. Clues don't come out and bite you. You have to go in after them."

Sam couldn't stand the arguing. "Hey, you two, if you keep it up, I'm going back and leaving you both stranded here." She indicated the disk in her hand. "Make up your minds, and let's do something. This wind is doing a number on my hair, not to mention the sand drying my eyes and throat."

Before either man could respond, the door of Piefenberg Laboratories opened, and a heavyset man came out.

"That's Lou Piefenberg, I think," Greg said. "Jane talked about him often. He's the owner and head scientist at the lab. It's been in his family for generations. He used to tell her they were on the verge of a cancer cure."

"So, they invented time travel instead and a way of bringing back the bubonic plague." Montmart still wore his fighting gloves.

"Shhh!" Greg said. "Let's see what Piefenberg's up to."

The heavy man in the white lab coat took a cigarette and lighter out of his left pocket and lit up.

"Wonderful. He smokes, too. He's probably trying to cure cancer, so he can save his own life."

"I told you to be quiet, Montmart."

171

Sam couldn't believe the behavior of the men. "Stop it, Please! I think there's someone else behind that door. Look!"

The trio riveted their eyes toward the lab door Piefenberg had just exited. From their vantage point behind one of the cactuses that lined the walkway to the building, they could see relatively well without being seen themselves. The door opened again and none other than Jane Oldsfield joined the doctor.

"I've been looking for you, Lou." Her voice was as smooth as sandpaper. "I think I've isolated those chemicals we were discussing. We may have a discovery here."

"That's it," Greg whispered. "She's talking about Rayore. We've come at exactly the right time."

"And what does that mean? Do we blow the place up?" Montmart's voice, always gravelly, sounded hoarser with the sand particles they were all inhaling.

"No. I told you. The past can't be changed. Rayore has to be invented. It's the disk we're after."

It was Sam's time to comment. "But if the compound was just invented now, won't it take Jane a while to create the disk before she hides it?"

"Time is relative in Oldsfield's game, Sam." She couldn't tell if Greg was squinting because of sand in his eyes or because he was scrutinizing the pair outside the lab. "Remember that the Jane you see isn't the past Jane; it's the future one. She's only here to make sure Piefenberg realizes his find. She probably has the future time disk on her right now."

"Now you've lost me," Sam said. "I realize that a future and past person can exist at the same time as RoseAnn did when we went back to ensure that her past self was murdered. But now you're saying that a future person can take a past person's place and not affect time."

"If it's Jane Oldsfield, it can be done. Remember, she's from a future time to begin with. What we really have to watch out for is if the Oldsfield from our time comes back and stops us from stopping the Oldsfield from this time's future. Then we're in real trouble."

Montmart made a sound that could've been a snort of disgust but didn't comment. Sam saw his hand start to fidget. She was afraid he was going to lose it any minute. She didn't have much of a chance to dwell on this, though, because a movement from behind their Saguaro cactus made them all jump, something a pin could've done at that moment.

"You've always been one step ahead of me, Greg," came the voice that sounded like an echo of the one outside the Piefenberg lab. "Too bad you hesitate so much. If you were as impatient as Montmart, you might have actually stopped me. Now I have no choice but to send the three of you through time while I finish my job here."

As Jane took the time travel disk out of the pocket of the identical black dress that her other self was wearing, Greg whispered to Sam, "When she aims that thing at us, take our disk and run. Try to find the one she's hidden and destroy it." He let go of her hand just as Jane fired a silver streak of light from the disk she held. Sam watched in horror as the light engulfed Greg and Philip, and they disappeared into granules of blowing sand. She backed away, while Jane prepared her next shot. Before Jane could fire again, Sam ran. She felt like an open target in the desolate desert but didn't look back as she raced for the canyon walls ahead. Since the panorama of sky and desert around her remained, she figured that Oldsfield hadn't been able to transport her. But what about Greg and Philip? To what time period had they been sent? How would they get back now without the time-travel disk she was holding? And how could she accomplish the task Greg had asked her to when she wasn't even sure the other time-travel disk was hidden here?

Sam paused to take a breath and peek behind her as she moved into the shadows of the hills. Having been an Eastern girl all her life, Sam hadn't known how awesome the desert mountains of the west could be. They were beautiful and terrorizing at the same time. A wild bird, possibly an endangered species, called out above her as it flew from one of the valley's peaks to the other. Sam shivered in the sudden coldness of the mountains, but her pursuer was nowhere in sight. Through the canyon wall, she saw a refraction of light. A shiny object was wedged between two orange rocks. She hoped it was the disk. She scrambled up the hill, nearly losing her footing as she hurried forward. She felt time pressing against her, its heavy weight holding her back as she took each higher step. At the top of the hill, she paused looking down from the dizzying height at the pebbles that had slid to the bottom. She felt like one of those pebbles — that at any moment she might fall to her fate, an insignificant digression in time's path.

She forced these thoughts from her mind as she reached for the glowing object sheltered between the two highest rocks. Her fingers brushed the tiny buttons while she carefully removed the disk from its lodging. She held her breath when the time-travel apparatus slipped into her cupped hands. She knew she had to destroy it.

She could toss it down the hill hoping it would break upon impact with the ground below or knock it against the rocks surrounding her until its microchips shattered into harmless pieces. She only knew she had to act soon before her stalker caught up with her.

The disk felt pounds heavier as she raised it toward the rock from where she'd extracted it. The first blow made a tiny dent on the left side; the second cracked off part of the turning wheel. Buoyed by newfound momentum, Sam pounded the disk against the rock until pieces of it flew off, one cutting into the side of her palm. Bleeding from the wound, she didn't stop.

The final blow Sam administered to the tiny machine caused her to stumble backward. She dropped the broken disk as she fell, grabbing one of the rocks she'd used as a foothold on her way up the hill. Her right hand was bleeding badly now as the rock she grasped tore open the scratch from the disk. As she groped her way to a standing position, she felt a tremor ride up the hill. Had her fall dislodged enough rock to cause an avalanche? It would only be ironic that she dies trying to save her future.

As she looked down, bracing herself against the side of the canyon, she heard a loud buzzing from where the last piece of the disk had fallen. A red glow a hundred times brighter than that which had alerted her to the hiding place of the disk, shone at the bottom. The buzzing grew louder – so loud she had to cover her ears. Blood dripped from the open wound on her hand to her neck and the front of her blouse's ripped shoulder. The buzzing glow throbbed through her, alternating in rhythms like a highly charged, blinking strand of Christmas tree lights. She felt faint. If it went on much longer, she was sure she would fall to her death.

CHAPTER TWENTY

"Time is the longest distance between two places."

— TENNESSEE WILLIAMS – *THE GLASS
MENAGERIE*

As Sam slid toward a reflecting pool that suddenly appeared in the middle of the desert, an oasis she thought she was imagining, an object caught on the belt buckle around the waist of her jeans that stopped her fall. She looked down to see the time disk that had transported her, Greg, and Philip to the scene of Rayore's discovery. She must've dropped it as she was destroying its duplicate from the past. The disk had lodged between a rock and a twig branch, giving just enough leverage to support her. She dug her bloody hands into the earth and clung there. She felt weak, drained from the force of time that she didn't have the strength to pull herself back up the hill.

As she lay, afraid and unable to move, she glanced down at the water below. In the blue ripples, different scenes played out in front of her like a wavy movie screen or a television set that needed its settings adjusted. The first scene featured herself and an old woman she recognized as her grandmother Emily, who'd died seven years ago of a sudden stroke. Sam had just come home from college the day her mother got the call. Mrs. Stewart responded to the news with chest pains instead of tears. She asked Sam to take care of all the details of the wake and funeral because she'd be too sick to attend. The memories flooded back, as Sam looked down at herself looking into the eyes of the woman who'd always been a ray of sunshine in the midst of her mother's thunderstorms. Emily Ballard had worked well into her seventies as a kindergarten teacher all her students loved because she loved them. She was crazy about children, although she and her husband only had Sam's mother. Robert Ballard died in his mid-fifties of a heart attack leaving Emily the house and a life-insurance policy to maintain it which she did lovingly and with thoughts of Sam's grandfather every day.

Emily Ballard spoke to Sam's reflection, and her voice echoed across the pool and off the canyon walls. "I've missed you, Sam. Remember all the fun we used to have when you were young, and your mother dropped you off at my house while she was at the doctors? Do you still remember how to make those ginger-bread cookies we baked for the holidays, or those pretty dresses for your dolls that I taught you to sew?"

"Yes, Granny." The words were out of Sam's mouth at the same time her reflection said them. She felt like a ventriloquist's puppet, or was her reflection the puppet – and she the ventriloquist?

"I'm so glad we could see each other again after all this time," her grandmother said. "I didn't want to leave you without saying goodbye, but sometimes it happens that way. Is your mother okay? I worry about her. I always did – maybe too much."

Sam felt dizzy, disoriented. Was this really her grandmother who was speaking to her? "Why are you here?" she asked, the words mixing with her reflection's.

"To save you, my dear." The blue eyes twinkled beneath the

wrinkled brow. "Give me the time-travel disk, and you can go back to your friends. I can send you back."

"How?" Sam felt even more confused. When she gazed away from the reflecting pool or looked up, she found it hard to breathe, as if the air was growing thinner above her, as if the water and its inhabitants were drawing her in.

"Just take the disk and place it in my hand." Sam's reflection was gone, and only her grandmother stood in the waters that were now crystal clear. She held out her thin hand. Sam wanted to go, but some sense, some instinct for survival, stopped her.

"I can't, Granny."

"Then I must go." The water began to ripple, as the reflection of her grandmother faded. "Take care of yourself, Sammy. I love you."

Tears formed in Sam's eyes as she watched Emily dissolve into the water. Had she done the wrong thing? But if she'd gone with her grandmother, would she have been saved or would she have joined her in death? And how could she be sure it was actually her grandmother she'd seen and not another of Jane Oldsfield's cunning tricks?

Sam's head began to throb as a migraine threatened. Soft raindrops fell on her, cooling her sweat-drenched body. After a few minutes, the drops fell faster and steadier, changing from small rivulets on the water to great splashes that wet the souls of her muddy sneakers and drenched her socks and lower pant legs. The wind was picking up also, whipping her drenched hair around her face. What was happening? Sam vaguely recalled reading an article in a travel magazine ages ago that described the violence of rainstorms in the desert. But then she noticed that the pattern of the rain had changed. The water was no longer falling from the sky but spewing forth from the reflecting pool. The storm was emanating from the depths of the water below her!

As Sam struggled to free a strand of hair from her left eye, the rain stopped as abruptly as it had started and a bright, warm light, brighter and hotter than any sunshine she'd ever seen or felt, shone over the now calm waters. Like a spotlight, a circle of brightness gathered in the center of the reflecting pool, and there at center stage stood her sister, Jennifer and her best friend, Angie. There was a third figure also, a little girl with red curly hair and a smile that displayed dimpled cheeks. The little girl stood next to Jennifer, and Sam thought there was a resemblance but couldn't identify the child.

"Hello, Sis." Her sister spoke. "I guess I should be happy you were the one who screwed up this time, but I'm not. I didn't die in that car crash. In fact, it never happened. You prevented it in a roundabout sort of way."

Before Sam could reply, Angie interrupted in her usual blunt manner. "My future was altered also by what your sister did. What you did, Sam." She looked up. "Mark and I put off having that first child, and we now have three healthy ones. The youngest one is best friends with this little girl. Do you know who she is, Sam?"

The redheaded girl, who Sam judged to be about three years old, stepped forward. The light shone on her alone. "It's me, Mommy," the girl said. "Aunt Jennifer and Aunt Angie want me to ask you to give them the disk. They said it's very important. Will you, Mommy, please?"

Sam looked into pleading brown eyes so much like her own. *I can't. You don't exist. You may never exist.* To the toddler in the pool, she said, "I'm sorry, honey. I have to protect this with my life."

"Even if that means you give up our lives." The light was on her sister. "How selfish can you be, Sam? Even if you don't save me. Even if you throw your future away. How can you deny your own daughter the life she was meant to live?"

The little girl began to cry, and the pitiful sound bounced off the water, echoing in Sam's ears. Angie picked up the child and tried to dry her tears. "Don't cry, Rosie. Your mom doesn't understand. There's an evil woman named Jane out there, and your mom is the only one who can stop her. But she has to let us help her. She has to trust us." She turned to look back up at Sam. "For the sake of Rosie, please give me the disk, Sam. I'm your best friend. I wouldn't hurt you for anything in the world. Please believe me."

"I can't, Angie. I don't know what's happening. I don't know whether you're real or just some scheme Jane concocted to get the disk."

"We're real," Jennifer said, stepping into the spotlight next to Angie and Rosie. "Ask me anything from our childhood. I'll know it. Go ahead, Sam. Let me prove I'm your sister."

Sam was wavering but forced herself to be strong. "You'd know all the answers if you could travel around in time like Jane Oldsfield."

"You always were too sensible, my friend, and even more stubborn than me." Angie put Rosie down. The child had stopped crying but was still looking at Sam with her pleading eyes. "What's happening here is that you're in a time warp. You're able to interact with people from your past and future. The people are real, Sam, the past and future, not necessarily. Your current time is frozen. That happened when you destroyed the disk Jane buried. What you need to do is go forward in time at least one minute past the time you destroyed the disk. But, in order to do that, you have to first go back in time one minute before you destroyed the disk, set the coordinates on your time-travel disk to one minute past the time you destroyed it, destroy the disk, and send yourself one minute forward in time before you're stuck in the time warp. The problem is that, while you're in the time warp, you can't use the time-travel disk, but we can."

Sam felt her headache returning, or had it ever gone? Could Angie be telling the truth? Was her only hope for survival, trust? "If what you say is true, I'll be stuck here forever unless I let you send me back."

"I'm afraid so, Sam. So, will you give us the disk now? There isn't much time. The warp is already beginning to change."

Sam saw what Angie was referring to. The pool was starting to ripple again as the two women and one young girl were beginning to fade from its surface.

Rosie's hand suddenly came up through the water. "Give me the disk, Mommy. Please. Hurry."

Sam dug frantically at the rock around the disk she'd been holding onto so tightly for what seemed like forever. But no matter how she tried, she didn't have the strength to loosen it. As her future daughter's hand descended back into the pool, Sam heard the girl's weak cries as she was swallowed up into the water, a tiny droplet in the ocean of tomorrow. "I'm sorry, Rosie," she cried. Then she thought. Rosie! Could that be short for RoseAnn? But, no, wasn't Greg the one she was destined for?

Sam's headache intensified as she grew weaker. Each change in the time warp seemed to drain her, as if her past and future were tugging at her in an exhausting match of strength. She closed her eyes to rest and felt as if she was falling asleep when a sucking sound startled her awake. It came from the reflecting pool. Sam looked down at the water receding into the earth. It was as if someone were siphoning out a swimming pool after the summer season. She watched in amazement as the water drained into the earth and all that remained was a crater of muddy dirt. Tiny buds appeared next, small green sprouts spreading across the circle, filling in the empty hole. Sam was astonished to watch the metamorphosis as the sprouts grew into grass so thick and lush they became a forest in the middle of the desert. Two of the sprouts on opposite sides grew into towering trees right before her eyes.

As Sam was admiring the change in the scenery, a man appeared from the west behind one tree at the same time another appeared from the east behind the other. They walked at the same pace to the center of the clearing where they addressed Sam.

"We're back," Greg said. "Jane temporarily transported us to your apartment. Floppy and Holly were there. They're both okay. But I had another disk to send us back here. Unfortunately, we got stuck in the time warp, too. Are you okay?"

"Does she look okay?" Philip asked. "She's clinging to a mountain, for God's sake! Sam, we can't reach you from the time warp. But if you could throw us your disk, maybe Parsons can get us the hell outta here. He should've listened to me in the first place when I suggested we blow up the lab."

"Don't go there, Montmart." Greg's reply was sharp. "It won't help matters now. Sam, we need your disk. Can you remove it from the rock?"

"No. I tried before. It seems to be stuck. What should I do?"

"Try again." Greg's tone was softer now. "Please, sweetheart, our future depends on it."

Montmart made a sound that was almost a snort. "Why are you so sure of yourself, Parsons? Just because you saw some possible preview of a future with Sam doesn't mean it's going to happen. You don't even know what real love is. Just look at your previous involvement — Jane Oldsfield. Talk about poor judgment. I can offer Sam so much more. I'd treasure and protect her."

"Protect her?" Greg laughed. "You did a real good job of protecting RoseAnn. What makes you think you'll do better with Sam?"

Sam couldn't believe they were arguing about petty jealousy at a time like this. "Please, guys, there isn't time for this right now." She was pushing and pulling on the disk between the rocks. "Ouch. I'm trying to dislodge the disk."

"Why don't you give her a hand, Parsons? You're such a hero."

"I'll give you a hand, you coward," Greg retorted. Suddenly, the two men were at blows. Sam wasn't sure who raised the first fist, but she thought it might've been Philip.

"Please, stop!" As she cried out, she yanked the disk harder, and it practically fell out of its lodging and down the embankment. She grabbed the sliding disk and exclaimed, "I've got it. Greg, Philip, I've got the disk!"

Neither man seemed to hear her as they rolled in the grass fighting their own private battle. They didn't even stop when a pair of black, three-inch high heels stepped beside them, and its owner shot a flare of light toward them from the disk she carried. The two men rolled apart as the streak of light hit them like a bolt of lightning. The grass on which they'd rolled turned from green to brown, then red, as flames spread over its dry surface.

Sam knew how devastating the spread of forest fires could be, but she'd never experienced one firsthand before. She screamed in horror as Greg and Phil tried in vain to escape the flames but were engulfed in seconds within its roaring blaze. Jane Oldsfield, looking on with a smile the size of the Cheshire Cat's, approached the mountain where Sam lay gripping the time-travel disk in her dirty and bloody hands.

"With your buddies out of the way, it's your turn, my dear," she said. Somehow, she'd escaped the flames and was climbing the mountain with surprising dexterity considering her clothing and shoes.

As the flames spread below in what had originally been the reflecting pool when the time warp first opened, Sam had little time to think about what was happening. She could no longer see Greg or Phillip. She couldn't believe they were actually gone. But if this were still a time warp, were they? If she could return to the moment prior to when she destroyed the hidden disk and send herself forward in time without opening the time warp, she might be able to prevent Greg and Philip's fiery deaths.

Oldsfield approached quickly. The woman didn't even seem out of breath as she scaled the mountain. It took Sam all of her remaining strength to scramble up the hill away from her. Somehow, Sam was able to pull herself up until she was standing on top of the mountain watching the fire scavenge the land below.

When she finally established firm footing on the ledge, Sam examined the disk trying to remember how to manipulate its buttons. The tiny device felt as heavy as a lead weight against her bruised palm. As Jane mounted the cliff, the disk seemed to gravitate toward her like a magnet, making it difficult for Sam to hold on to.

"I'm sorry you have to learn this lesson the hard way," Jane said pulling the disk from Sam's trembling grasp. "If you'd listened to me instead of Greg, your future would've been so much brighter."

"No," Sam yelled as she grabbed Oldsfield's sleeve. "Give me that back."

The two women struggled on the side of the mountain as the pit of fire burned beneath them and flames climbed the rocks. At one point the disk was in danger of hurtling down into the burning valley but was reclaimed by Jane as Sam lost her footing and started to fall.

CHAPTER TWENTY-ONE

"There are many events in the womb of time which will be delivered."

— SHAKESPEARE - *OTHELLO*

A s Sam fell, she suddenly stopped midway down the mountain and halfway toward the flaming pit. Suspended in air, she felt as if she'd been sucked into a vacuum. Numbers flew around her, and she began to recognize them as years counting forward from her birth year, 1966, until the present, 1998. Along with the numbers came images, and she thought her life was flashing in front of her before she died, but the images she was viewing weren't from her history but from the world's.

As 1967 flew by, she saw people dressed in bell bottom pants, women with flowers in their hair, men with long hair and beards, and recognized the hippies known as "flower children." She saw the gathering at Woodstock and protestors waving signs, "Make Peace, not War." When 1969 flew by, she heard the song, "Age of Aquarius." Then she recognized the familiar broadcast of the Moonwalk as Neil Armstrong made history by placing a flag on the moon and saying, "That's one small step for man. One giant leap for mankind."

The numbers began to fly by faster. They paused in 1974, where she saw Nixon being impeached for Watergate. In 1981, she saw homosexuals, drug addicts, and blood recipients dying from AIDS. The numbers flashed by faster, and she saw a news broadcast from the previous year of Princess Diana's tragic death in a Paris car crash.

Then the numbers started to slow as she viewed images from the future. In 1999, she read newspaper headlines featuring the term "Y2K" and predicting the shutdown of the world's computers as the century changed. As 2001 flashed before her, she saw people running across a bridge and recognized the Twin Towers in New York City crumbling before her eyes. This horrific scene morphed into a space shuttle exploding in the air in 2003. Then she saw people talking into a device they carried around with them in 2007. The 2008 presidential election featured a black man named Barack Obama winning office. Then she felt a terrible wind blowing around her as 2012 brought sights of homes being destroyed and trees knocked down. Her future view ended in 2020 when she saw people huddled in their homes wearing face masks. Signs on businesses read, "Closed due to the pandemic."

After those scenes played before her, Sam waited for the next year to appear dreading what other disaster or horror she'd witness, but no further numbers appeared. Whatever time warp she'd been suspended in seemed to dissolve, and she felt herself begin to fall again toward the fiery pit. She closed her eyes and prayed that the end would come quickly and painlessly, but instead of continuing her descent, her direction was reversed, and the magnetic-type pull that had gripped her now lifted her back up so that she stood once again on the mountain with the fire roaring upwards as Jane tapped out coordinates on the time-travel disk.

Sam knew she only had seconds to act, but the flames were

now just inches beneath her toes. She stumbled forward, ignoring the crunch of rocks that fell into the fire in her wake. She was fingertips from Oldsfield when a savage sound startled both of them. Jane dropped the disk as two flying felines simultaneously landed on her shoulders from the rocks above. The disk fell into Sam's open hands.

Jane threw the cats off with a violent shrug that knocked her forward down the mountain. She didn't even have time to scream as she fell into the fiery pit.

Sam, exhausted, leaned against the ledge to which Floppy and Holly were clinging. "Where in the world did you two come from?" she asked. Then she had a thought. If, before he was engulfed in flames, Greg or Philip, whichever one was holding their time disk, had been able to send the cats to the same coordinates …

The desert wind was picking up as the flames billowed closer. "I guess we should go now," Sam said. Glancing at the disk, she made adjustments remembering how Greg had instructed her in its setting. "I hope this is right." She gave both cats a pet, took a paw in each hand, and pressed what she hoped were the proper sequence of buttons on the disk.

CHAPTER TWENTY-TWO

"All we have to decide is what to do with the time given to us."

— J.R.R. TOLKIEN

S am was in exactly the same spot on the mountain, but no cats purred beside her and no flames roared below.

Through the canyon wall, Sam saw a refraction of light. A shiny object was wedged between two orange rocks. Could she hope it was the disk, the original one that she'd destroyed before the time warp opened? She scrambled up the hill, almost losing her footing as she hurried forward. She felt time pressing against her, its heavy weight holding her back as she took each higher step. At the top of the hill, she paused looking down from the dizzying height at the pebbles that had slid to the bottom. She thought about Greg and Phil, RoseAnn, and the child she might've had. She also thought of the future events that she'd seen and wondered if they'd come to pass and if she'd ever know.

She forced these thoughts from her mind as she reached for the glowing object sheltered between the two highest rocks. Her fingers brushed the tiny buttons while she carefully removed the disk from its lodging. She held her breath when the time-travel apparatus slipped into her cupped hands. She knew she had to destroy it and then send herself ahead in time before the time warp engulfed her with its unclear predictions and ominous picture show.

Emotionally, as well as physically, Sam was drained. But she summoned up the last bit of strength she had to beat the disk against the hillside until tiny pieces flew off. Bit by bit, microchip by microchip, the deadly device disintegrated in this microcosmic battle between machine and human. When Sam flung the last remaining piece down the mountain, she felt both satisfaction and a strange sense of sadness, but she had no time to contemplate the results of her actions. With trembling, raw, and bloody hands, she retrieved her own disk and set it forward one minute, then pressed the center button and whispered a prayer.

The feeling of time transference enveloped Sam in a whirlwind so strong she felt faint. Whether traveling forward or backward in time, past or behind a second or a century, the pull of time was more akin to a tug-of-war than a seesaw slide. Sam held her breath and closed her eyes against the shifting tide.

A sudden movement jolted her awake. Sam stared at the sight before her, familiar yet foreign. A small oak table, bare except for an opened newspaper spread across its surface. A half-open window curtained with blue gingham on which rested a gray, rather fat cat who'd turned his gaze from the Manhattan skyline to the object of the movement that had jumped onto the table and was now covering Sam's reading material with a red striped paw.

"Holly, Floppy! I'm back," Sam exclaimed finally realizing the meaning of Dorothy's motto, "there's no place like home." She glanced down at the paper where Holly's paw marked a box in the help wanted column of the classified section. It was the ad for the job at Virtual Software that she'd first seen two weeks ago. But how could that be? If she'd sent herself forward in time, how had she'd ended up in the past? And what was Floppy doing here?

Before Sam could attempt to answer any of her own questions, the bell to her apartment rang from downstairs. She got up, dislodging Holly and the paper in the same sweep and ran to answer it with both cats following at her heels.

As she passed Mr. Clancy's door, she thought of the old man briefly and how she'd like to invite him for another spaghetti dinner one day soon. She felt giddy suddenly, as if she now owned her future. When she'd have time to reflect on it later, she'd probably compare the feeling to one that touches those who come close to death and live to tell about it.

Sam opened the door. Two men stood on the step smiling at her.

"You did it, Sam," Greg said.

"Without any help from us," Philip added.

"Maybe just a little from one of you," Sam purported as she rushed to hug them both in one large embrace as two furry faces watched from the alcove.

When the three released one another, Sam looked first into Greg's dark blue eyes and then into Philip's hazel ones, as she asked, "So, which one of you is it?" The question addressed multiple issues.

The men shrugged.

"Don't do this to me, guys."

"You have my cat," Greg said bending to rub the gray head of Floppy who'd scampered to his long-lost owner.

"But don't forget Rosie," Philip said. "She might be ours one day."

It was Sam's turn to smile. "Do either of you actually know?"

"Only the future knows," Greg replied.

Dear reader,

We hope you enjoyed reading *Time's Relative*. Please take a moment to leave a review, even if it's a short one. Your opinion is important to us.

Discover more books by Debbie De Louise at https://www.nextchapter.pub/authors/debbie-de-louise

Want to know when one of our books is free or discounted? Join the newsletter at http://eepurl.com/bqqB3H

Best regards,
Debbie De Louise and the Next Chapter Team

ACKNOWLEDGMENTS

I'd like to thank the fine staff at Next Chapter especially Miika Hannila who continues to find new ways to market and promote books worldwide. I'm thrilled that my Next Chapter books are available in a wide variety of formats including paperback, eBook, large print, audio, and hardcover with some translated into other languages, as well. I'd also like to acknowledge my fellow Next Chapter authors. I'm honored to be part of this team of talented writers.

Thanks also to my other author friends, my family, and all those who have supported my writing especially my readers who make all the hard work worthwhile. If you enjoy this book and any of my others, I would be grateful for a brief review on Amazon, Goodreads, your blog, and/or any of my social media sites.

ABOUT THE AUTHOR

Debbie De Louise is an award-winning author and a reference librarian at a public library on Long Island. She is a member of Sisters-in-Crime, International Thriller Writers, the Long Island Authors Group, and the Cat Writers' Association. Her novels include the five books and four stories of the Cobble Cove cozy mystery series, a comedy novella, *When Jack Trumps Ace*, a paranormal romance, *Cloudy Rainbow*, and the standalone mysteries; *Reason to Die, Sea Scope*, and *Memory Makers*. Debbie has also written a non-fiction cat book, *Pet Posts: The Cat Chats*, written from the points of view of four of her cats and has also published articles in online and print pet magazines including Catster.com.

Debbie's stories, poems, and essays appear in the Red Penguin Collections, *What Lies Beyond, 'Tis the Season, A Heart Full of Love, We Made It!, Stand Out*, and *The Roaring 20s: A Decade of Stories*. Her story, "The Birthday Gift" also appears in the Bloom Literary Magazine. Her poems are also featured in the Nassau County *Voices In Verse* 2020 anthology and the 2020 *Bards Annual*. She lives on Long Island with her husband, daughter, and three cats.

CONNECT WITH DEBBIE ON THE FOLLOWING SITES:

Website/Blog/Newsletter Sign-Up: https://debbiedelouise.com

Facebook: https://www.facebook.com/debbie.delouise.author/
Twitter: https://twitter.com/Deblibrarian
Goodreads: https://www.goodreads.com/author/show/
2750133.Debbie_De_Louise
Amazon Author Page: http://amzn.to/2bIHdaQ
All Author: https://allauthor.com/author/debbiedelouise/
Instagram: https://www.instagram.com/debbie_writer/
Linkedin: https://www.linkedin.com/in/debbiedelouise/
Bookbub: https://www.bookbub.com/profile/debbie-de-louise
Pinterest: https://www.pinterest.com/debbiedelouise
Debbie's Character's Chat Group: https://www.facebook.com/
groups/748912598599469/
Sneaky the Library Cat's blog: https://Sneakylibrarycat.word-
press.com

Made in the USA
Monee, IL
21 August 2021